The Devil's Country

The Devil's Country

Perla Suez

Translated by
Rhonda Dahl Buchanan

WHITE PINE PRESS / BUFFALO, NEW YORK

White Pine Press
PO Box 236
Buffalo, NY 14201
www.whitepine.org

Originally published by Editorial Edhasa, Ciudad Autónoma de Buenos Aires as *El país del diablo.*

Publication of this book was made possible, in part, with funds from the University of Louisville and under the auspices of work published within the framework of the "SUR" Translation Support Program of the Ministry of Foreign Affairs, International Trade and Worship of the Argentine Republic.

Printed and bound in the United States of America.

ISBN 978-1-945680-33-5

Library of Congress number 2018968434

For Roberto, Luciana, Laura, and Martín

Don't be sad; don't think I'm going to die.
I tell all of you this so you won't despair
and so you know that I'll become a machi.

—Testimony of a *Mapuche* girl*

Don't be savages, fence with barbed wire.

—Domingo F. Sarmiento**

* Pascual Coña, Lonco. *Testimonio de un cacique mapuche.* Santiago de Chile: Pehuén, Biblioteca del
    Bicentenario, 1984. p. 352.
** Rodríguez, Fermín A. *Un desierto para la Nación, la escritura del vacío.* Buenos Aires: Eterna Cadencia,
    2010. p. 190.

The Devil's Country

Translator's Preface

On December 2, 2015, at the International Book Fair in Guadalajara, Mexico, the Argentine writer Perla Suez received the 23rd Premio de Literatura Sor Juana Inés de la Cruz for her novel *El país del diablo* (Buenos Aires: Edhasa, 2015). Suez began her acceptance speech for this annual prize, which recognizes the best novel written in Spanish by a woman author, with the following words: "Authors are not interested in narrating glorious times but rather difficult and contradictory moments." Indeed, one of the most troublesome and contradictory moments of Argentine history serves as a backdrop for Suez's latest novel, which owes its title to General Julio Argentino Roca who, before assuming his first term as President of Argentina in 1880, led the Conquest of the Desert, a military campaign in the 1870s to exterminate the indigenous populations of the Pampas, an area he referred to as "*el país del diablo*," "the devil's country."

A fan of Quentin Tarantino films, Perla Suez refers to *The Devil's Country* as her "Patagonian western." However, unlike *Django Unchained*, there is little black humor to be found in this novel that unravels a tale of vengeance and vigilante justice at the hands of an unlikely heroine, a fourteen-year-old girl named Lum Hué, daughter of a white man and a *Mapuche* mother and sole survivor of the massacre of her village at the hands of white troops and Indian soldiers drafted by force into the army. Ironically, under President Roca, Argentina opened its doors to waves of European immigrants, among them Suez's ancestors, who sought refuge from the genocide of Russian Jews under

Czar Nicholas II and settled in the agricultural colonies of the Entre Ríos province. The author explains the impetus for writing the novel in the following way:

> General Roca said that the devil's country had to be eradicated, that its people had to be exterminated. I myself am the granddaughter of Europeans, and General Roca was the one who gave my grandparents a place to live, where they could make a living, where my parents could study, but I denounce the one who massacred indigenous communities in order to give land to my ancestors. Argentina would have been a much more amazing country with that multiplicity of cultures. In these terrible times when huge waves of refugees world-wide are searching for a place to live, I felt compelled to tell the story of that pain. (*"Perla Suez obtuvo el Premio,"* translation mine)

In an interview with Malena Rey, Suez reveals that the image of the desert has been engraved in her memory since her childhood, when her paternal grandfather, a rabbi known in Basavilbaso as *El Gaucho Froique,* told her tales of the exodus of Jews across the sands of the Sahara. One could say that with this latest novel, Suez constructs a bridge of sand between the desert of Patagonia and the desert of her ancestors:

> In my work, I've always returned to the same obsession: my ancestors escaping, my grandparents coming from Europe to Argentina by boat, and the theme of immigration in general. I know that with this latest novel, I somehow put to rest a topic that had obsessed me. When I explored the *Mapuche* (or *Araucano*) culture, I realized that it was not foreign to me. After all, the desert and the displaced tribes who searched thousands of years ago for a place to live exist in my roots too. "Desert" is one of the most important words I heard during my childhood when my paternal grandfather would tell me how my ancestors escaped from Egypt. (*"Las riendas del desierto,"* par. 3, translation mine)

In *The Devil's Country*, as in her previous five novels, Suez focuses on the private lives of marginalized individuals whose names do not appear in the official chronicles of Argentine history, but who, in one way or another, form part of the country's national identity. In the novels that comprise the *Entre Ríos Trilogy* (2006), Suez inserts crucial moments of Argentina's history into intimate family histories enacted on a smaller stage. While her first four novels take place in the Entre Ríos province, where she spent the first fifteen years of her life, the setting for *Humo rojo* (Buenos Aires: Edhasa, 2012) shifts to the Chaco province. *Red Smoke*, which garnered Suez the 2013 Premio Nacional de Novela, discloses the unethical practices that the Anglo-Argentine company *La Forestal* employed in the 1930s and 1940s to seize territory of the owners of charcoal kilns in the dense forest zone of the Chaco known as *El Impenetrable*. In the process, the author reveals the absolute indifference toward indigenous laborers who were forced to remain submissive and silent in the face of abuse.

Suez, in *The Devil's Country*, strays even further from her native province of Entre Ríos to Patagonia and highlights the plight of the indigenous *Mapuche* communities whose territory is taken from them. A recurring theme in Suez's fiction is the role that violence and authoritarianism has played throughout Argentina's history, particularly the imposition of power over the weak and defenseless. In *The Devil's Country*, Suez inverts the paradigm of civilization vs. barbarism first proposed by another Argentine president, Domingo Faustino Sarmiento, in his classic book *Facundo: Civilization and Barbarism*. In an interview with Roberto Estrada, Suez explains that in school they were taught the whites were civilized and the Indians were the barbarians, an arbitrary dichotomy that she overturns in this novel (*"Un desierto sin bárbaros"*).

Suez explains her desire to disclose the truth concealed by the official story taught to generations of Argentines:

> I wrote this novel so that I could understand the culture of the *Mapuche* people who inhabited the part of the Argentine Patagonia where the so-called Conquest of the Desert took place. Over and over I asked myself who were the civilized ones and who were the barbarians, and I felt the need to expose what they never told me. Fiction helped me unearth another story, and that is what I

attempted to write in *The Devil's Country*. (Rey, par. 3, translation mine)

Before the reader enters the narrative world that Suez creates in this novel, two epigraphs allude to the clash of cultures that is about to ensue. Suez chose the following words by Sarmiento as the second epigraph: "Don't be savages, fence with barbed wire," a quotation that reflects the vast differences in attitude that the native communities and the invaders had toward the land. While the *Mapuches* considered themselves to be privileged caretakers of the sacred and boundless land, those who invaded the Patagonian desert only valued the land for its economic potential, proclaiming victory over conquered territory with *mojones*, or boundary markers. Deus, the French surveyor and photographer who documents the conquests of the troops, recognizes the important role that barbed-wire fencing will play in establishing order and progress in the rural territories of the developing nation. In the following passage, Deus explains to Rufino, one of the soldiers, that the process of taming the land began in 1845, thirty years before the Conquest of the Desert, coincidentally the very same year that Sarmiento published his groundbreaking book *Facundo: Civilization and Barbarism*:

> It was in 1845, I believe, when they brought the barbed wire from England. Now it's a widely-used method in the rural areas that lends order to this country hounded by barbarians. The most progressive ranch owners erected barbed-wire fences before they planted thorny *espino* shrubs or placed boundary markers. The transformation of the *pampas* will be slow, but that's how the cattle industry and foreign investment will grow more rapidly, and the country will develop.
>
> Nothing's wasted if it's fenced in. It's a necessary investment, proclaims the photographer.
>
> These Indians never knew how to manage the land or profit from it. (p. 69)

It is worth noting that the first campaign to exterminate the indigenous communities of Patagonia and appropriate their territory for ranchers was organized in 1833 by Juan Manuel de Rosas, the Governor of the Province of Gran Buenos Aires. Although this campaign took place four decades before General Roca's Conquest of the Desert, allusions to Rosas, whose federalist regime ruled Argentina until his exile in 1852, appear throughout the novel. For example, there are references to a coveted knife engraved with the initials J. R. M., which once belonged to *El Restaurador,* or the Restorer of the Laws, as Rosas was known. There are also allusions to the red armbands that were to be worn to indicate support for the Federalists, and the color blue worn by the opposition, the Unitiarians. In the vicious battle for power between Unitarians and Federalists, Rosas relied on the *Mazorca,* a brutal police force whose favorite tactic for eliminating enemies was to behead them, slicing their necks back and forth with a long blade as if playing a violin. A reference to this macabre practice of severing heads of the "savages" with a *"violín y violón,"* appears on the final page of the novel.

The first epigraph of the novel is also revealing and alerts the reader to the pivotal role that a young girl will play in the story they are about to read. Suez chose for this epigraph the words of a *Mapuche* girl that appear in a book called *Testimony of a Mapuche Chief:* "Don't be sad; don't think I'm going to die. I tell all of you this so you won't despair and so you know that I'll become a *machi.*" Oftentimes in Suez's narrative fiction, justice is served at the hands of an adolescent character, frequently a young girl, as is the case in *Complot* (2004), the third novel of the *Entre Ríos Trilogy.* The protagonist of *The Devil's Country* is a young *mestiza* whose name, Lum, means "convergence of two lagoons" in the *Mapuche* language, a fitting name for a biracial girl who suffers from feelings of alienation and struggles to fulfill her true destiny as a medicine woman.

The novel unfolds at a vertiginous pace, not unlike the familiar scenes of hot pursuit so common in many Western films. It is no coincidence that Suez incorporates cinematographic techniques in *The Devil's Country* and her previous novels, given that she studied cinematography in the 1960s. With a minimalist prose that has become the trademark of her narrative fiction, Suez reconstructs a journey of revenge and justice, utilizing a number of discursive techniques, such as diaries and letters, incantations and prayers, dreams and visions, and flashbacks and fast forwards to capture the thoughts, fears, and hopes of a young girl and the soldiers whose actions changed the fate of Lum, her people, and ultimately the nation.

This novel pieces together the story of a young girl who summons the courage to avenge the massacre of her people and the destruction of her village and to continue alone on her journey to fulfill her destiny as a *machi*. Just as a young girl comes of age and takes her place in society, so too a nation forges its identity, a steady passage from one era to the next that is marked by violence. Ultimately, in this novel, Suez raises the question that is at the heart of Argentina's tumultuous history: Who are the civilized and who are the barbarians? Although this novel takes place during the second half of the nineteenth century in the *pampas* of Argentina's Patagonia, the hatred and fear of the other and the violence that erupts because of intolerance toward cultural differences is very relevant today, not only in Latin America but in all other continents of the world as well. Readers of *The Devil's Country* will recognize universal themes related to genocide, immigration, assimilation, and racial discrimination that have become the fodder of international news, in addition to other sub-themes, such as respect for nature and the land, and the value of preserving rituals and traditions. The novel's setting and time period may be remote, but the issues are current, and the reader will perceive in Perla Suez's characters the basic weaknesses of human nature that may lead to destruction, as well as the triumph of the human spirit to overcome social injustice.

—Rhonda Dahl Buchanan

Works Cited:

Estrada, Roberto. "Un desierto sin bárbaros." *La Gaceta de la Universidad de Guadalajara.* 9 Nov. 2015.

"Perla Suez obtuvo el Premio Sor Juana por *El país del diablo.*" *Noticias de la FIL* [Guadalajara, México] 3 Nov. 2015.

Rey, Malena. "Las riendas del desierto." *Página 12* [Buenos Aires] 31 Dec. 2015.

Suez, Perla. *El país del diablo.* Buenos Aires: Edhasa, 2015.

—. Acceptance Speech for the Premio Sor Juana Inéz de la Cruz. Feria del Libro Internacional. Guadalajara, Mexico. 2 December 2015.

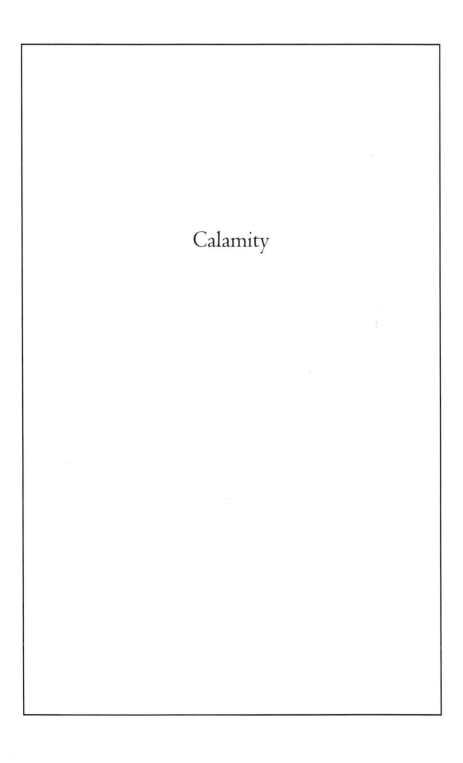

Calamity

A massive contingent of soldiers has been dispatched into the void. White men and Indians advance like an army of trained fleas. Wagon wheels spin rapidly as they forge ahead. Mules laden with firearms keep pace. As they infiltrate the devil's country, the desert bears witness to this defining moment.

A Rite of Passage

It's still dark in the early hours of the new day as the *machi* makes her way with short steps through the tall grasses. In her left hand, she raises the ceremonial drum on which the universe is drawn, divided into four parts with symbols of heaven and earth. She beats the *cultrún* with her right hand. The medicine woman wears a necklace with long rows of silver discs joined at the center by a two-headed eagle, and a headband to hold back her thick black hair, peppered with white strands. A colorful wool poncho, fastened at the neck with a brooch, falls over her shoulders.

The fourteen-year-old Indian girl, who is about to be initiated, walks ahead of her with a torch raised high to light the way. She wears a plain, light brown wool tunic, cinched at the waist with a sash, and her unruly dark hair escapes her headband, unrestrained like a horse's mane. She has the broad back of the *Araucanos* and almond-shaped eyes, deep-set as if etched with a knife. But her eyes are the color of honey, and blotchy patches of skin expose a fairness she tried to conceal with the help of the sun.

A group of men and women follows, sixteen members of the tribe, all carrying torches. They chant and drink *chicha,* and some dance, spinning round and clapping as they cross the damp grasslands and head toward a hill.

They come to a hollow where a wooden totem rises four meters in the midst of the *rehue,* the sacred place of rebirth, an area covered in vegetation, apple and *maqui* trees, and *quila* grasses. In the center stands a log carved with seven steps, the last two engraved with a human head and a hat. The first step represents wholeness, the second wisdom, the third tradition, the fourth labor, the fifth justice, the sixth freedom, and the seventh, at the top, symbolizes the people. It faces east to mark the passage of the day, the birth of the sun, the changing seasons, and represents man standing on one point of the planet.

The group forms a circle and sticks their torches into the ground. They continue singing and dancing, while a few women prepare a bed with blankets for the girl to lie down. The old *machi* puts down the drum and approaches her disciple, who has already removed her tunic. She keeps chanting as she takes some small bags from a satchel and places them around the girl. Then from her leather bag, she pours a little *chicha* into some pots. Next, the old woman begins to scrape the skin of the girl's arms and legs with a sharp-edged stone, following ancient ritual, so that the novice may be reborn with new skin after the ceremonial death of initiation. The other women surround her, and their murmuring voices seem to isolate them from what remains of the night.

The *machi* takes some seeds from a leather pouch, grinds them in a mortar, and puts the powder in her pipe and lights it. The girl sits down on the bed, and the old woman passes her the pipe. After four or five puffs, she enters into a trance and her body goes limp. The *machi* extinguishes the pipe and sits on the ground to play her *cultrún* and sing, while the others form a circle around the totem, ringing bells to accompany their chants.

The girl rises and starts dancing to the beat of the drum, becoming more enraptured as the music builds. She moves toward the totem to complete her sacred journey, climbing the steps one by one and using her hands to reach the top of the *rehue*, where she stands tall, extends her arms, and gazes toward the sky, declaring:

I, Lum Hué, bear the number four in my being, the sacred number four that represents the essence of the universe and mankind, the rain, the sun that sleeps at night, the season of growth and abundance, and the time for rest. Inside me is the force of a lagoon hidden between two others, and that's why my element is water. I've been on this fertile earth fourteen years, and on this day, I'll become a machi.

From now on you'll live in me, Ngenechen, because you've chosen me. I'm not a machi

24

of my own will but because you've summoned me. They say you ride a beautiful horse and are surrounded by animals. Give me animals, too, as a reward for my labor. I'll be a perfect machi *and will not invoke the dark spirits or practice black magic. I'll be a good medicine woman who heals the sick, and our people will say that we'll no longer perish.*

Swaying and chanting, the girl raises her voice while the old *machi's* drum beats faster and faster. As she reaches spiritual ecstasy, she arches back and then bows down, crossing her arms over her chest before leaping. Everyone cheers, shouts, and encircles her, wanting to touch her. Two men lift her and place her on the bed. The medicine woman covers her with straw, leaving her to sleep and dream of the spirits who will visit her so that the young Indian girl may die and the new *machi* be born.

The group slits the throat of a ram they brought to sacrifice. By the light of the fire, the *machi* watches the blood spill and a series of images cross her mind, making her shudder and lose her balance. A burned *rehue*. Hands yanking a branch of the sacred *foike* tree. A wandering mare. Death. Her eyes roll back and turn white, and she hears the wind howling in her ears, speaking about her disciple and revealing her destiny, and there's nothing she can do.

As fear clouds the *machi's* face, a woman asks what she's seen. She looks at her with anguish and shakes her head in denial, refusing to tell her what makes no sense. The woman lends the old *machi* an arm and tells her not to worry, that the ceremony was a success and they will continue celebrating in the morning. The *machi* answers no, that the spirits have sent her a message. Then she lets go of the woman's arm, raises her hands, and asks everyone to listen.

The people gather round and the old woman tells them she's received instructions from the other world to leave the novice alone and allow other forces to care for her. She tells them it's not their place to interfere and they must return home and wait. When morning arrives, they'll know what Ngenechen commands, which is what matters most and no one can disobey. The men and women look at each other in distress, greatly disappointed that they can't abide by tradition and continue to celebrate and make their offerings, but the *machi* is adamant and they respect her too much to object. Slowly they gather their things and head back to the village.

The *machi* goes over to the young girl lying in a deep slumber and waves her hands in the air over her head and chest, whispering a prayer. Then she bends down and kisses her on the forehead, lingering a while longer. She's reluctant to leave her, but like someone who must obey an order, she takes a deep breath, gets up, and walks away.

The sun has yet to rise over the village. In her hut made of bulrush reeds, bamboo canes, and hides, the old *machi* lights a small fire. Ears of corn dangle from rods placed above the fire, herbs are hung to dry here and there, a sheep's skin covers the ground, and a stone for grinding toasted wheat sits on top of it. Scattered about the hut are cigars bought from the white men at the border, plates and wooden spoons, small rocks in different colors and shapes, dozens of clay pots and cups made from a ram's horn, and other objects.

Ngenechen, please allow her to see what lies beyond, the *machi* pleads.

She's alone and needs guidance so that the evil spirit and bad people no longer pursue her. Let a pale blue light settle in her body and mind and shine from within, and though most of our people can't see it, a few of the revered ones will. This girl came to me, and it was as if suddenly the roof of my hut had lifted. I told the chief even though some white blood may run through her veins, she's ours. Her gaze sees beyond the land and far into the sky. She's brave, loves music and animals, and has learned quickly which plants may be used for healing.

Ngenechen, you entrusted her to me, telling me to give her a new identity, following our sacred order to give her our words so they would become hers. It was then that I gave her the name Lum Hué.

The old *machi* is lost in thought while she crushes chili pepper, coriander seeds, and oregano in the mortar. As she seasons a piece of meat to grill, she hears a commotion and stops what she's doing and peers out.

It's happening now, she says with a solemn voice.

A man sounds the alarm. The soldiers are drawing near.

A Memory in a Trance

Lum and her mother are bathing in the river. The girl just spit out a tiny fish and her mother laughs. Fén stands up suddenly when she sees the white man appear on the shore. He motions her to get out of the water and she obeys.

Lum watches them from the river. She crouches until the water comes up to her chin, then dips her head slightly and blows out, forming bubbles.

Her mother begins to shout in the language of her father, and Lum doesn't understand what they're saying. She shivers, afraid he'll beat her mother again. Her father forces Fén to kneel before him, and she fights back and tries to stand, but he pushes her down again and she falls to her knees. With a wild look on his face, he draws his saber, yanks her by the hair, and with one swift movement cuts off her head. When he lets go, the head falls and rolls on the ground like a ball of rags until it reaches the shoreline.

Lum sees him walking to the water. She remains still and silent in the middle of the riverbed as her father washes the steel blade, knowing she's watching him. Then he returns the saber to its sheath and turns around. He walks over to where he tied his horse, mounts, and leaves for good.

A trickle of blood makes its way to Lum from the other shore, and she stands up suddenly and runs. She holds her mother's head between her hands and tries to put it back on the body but it slips from her grasp. She picks it up again and begins to scream, wailing as she cradles it, and lies there, stretched out on the shore.

Ablaze

The fog conceals something in the distance. A throng of voices and horses neighing can be heard. A ram's horn sounds the alarm, but it's too late. The calvary descends upon the village, surging like an avalanche. Horses' hooves trample pots and bowls, quickly demolishing everything. People run from their huts trying in vain to save themselves from the deadly weapons. Screams, screeching voices, and dust fill the air. Soldiers from the border, haggard and filthy, pounce upon the Indians like hyenas. Hands and open arms are blown to bits.

The tribe's sentry leaps onto one of the enemy horses, brandishing his lance and knocking off the rider, leaving him impaled on the ground, a fleeting triumph as bullets fly in all directions and one pierces the Indian's back.

A woman grabs a clay pot full of boiling grease to defend herself, hurling it at the face of an officer. Her children hide behind her. Another soldier shoots her between the eyes and makes certain the children don't survive their mother.

A spear whistles as it pierces the wind, but misses the target in the battle that's nearly won. An Indian wearing a blue jacket has a rifle in his hand. He fires, leaving one more dead Indian. The *machi* stands outside her hut beating the *cultrún* to summon the spirits. Although her gaze is lost in the distance, the Indian soldier thinks she's staring at him and feels anxious in the midst of the massacre.

A soldier strikes an old man's head with the butt of his rifle, and he doubles over with blood running down his cheeks. The attacker takes the safety off his firearm and pulls the trigger as the old man stays on his knees, but he's out of bullets. The soldier calls another nearby who hands him some cartridges but doesn't wait for his comrade to load.

A shot rings out, and another and another and another.

A bullet enters one side of the *machi*'s torso and she collapses.

The huts are still burning at midday, and the blaze casts a bright light over the arid land. Visible under that glow are men on horseback, sheep, and wagons carrying away most of the troops and the rescued captive women.

Amidst the panting of animals and pounding hoofs, a man tries with all his might to breathe. A spear has pierced his chest and his hands are swollen from pain and poison. He wears an army uniform and his body shakes in spasms until he finally stops moving. Five men stand around him. The lieutenant takes a few draws from the stub of a cigarette stub as he observes the colonel's dying moments. Deus, the photographer, anxiously prepares one plate after another. Ancatril, the Indian soldier, prays in a crouched position. Carranza cleans his rifle without paying attention to the scene. Rufino is bored.

The lieutenant puts out his cigarette with the tip of his boot.

"Rest in peace, Ordóñez."

He bends over the dead colonel, closes his eyelids, unfastens the medals pinned to his jacket, and pins them onto his own.

Carranza looks at the lieutenant out of the corner of his eye.

"Damn, it's hotter than hell. In a few more hours this place is going to stink worse than the slaughterhouse, and it's already swarming with flies."

Rufino ignores Carranza and asks, "What are we going to do with his body, Lieutenant?"

"Bury him."

Rufino digs a hole in the softest part of the land. Then he rummages through Ordóñez's clothing searching for that knife with the silver handle and maroon-colored stone, engraved with the initials J.R.M., the one the colonel always liked to flaunt and boast about its priceless value, but it's nowhere to be found on the dead man. Someone's stolen it, probably the same imbecile who forgot to take the gold watch that Rufino hides in the lining of his jacket.

The photographer scurries over the area searching for someone worth photographing and comes across the old *machi*. He stops and stares at her and notices that the necklace adorning her chest seems to move rhythmically. She's still breathing. Carranza comes over, kicks the body with his boot, and unsheathes his knife, while the photographer looks on with fascination.

"Wait, Carranza, I'm going to get my equipment."

Deus fetches the crate with his camera, sets it up in front of the scene, inserts a plate, and instructs the soldier:

"Do it slowly because I have to expose it for a few seconds."

The sergeant bends over and sinks the knife slowly into the woman's chest, leaving it there as he poses with a smile until the photographer tells him to remove it. The Indian dressed in blue watches from a short distance, shedding a few tears that could be taken for sweat.

The lieutenant sees the *cultrún* lying near the *machi*'s body.

"This deserves to be in a museum. It's not just any old drum."

"If you hadn't been such butchers," he berates Deus and Carranza, "even the old woman could've been displayed in the Museum of Natural Sciences, and that would've made Perito Moreno happy."

The lieutenant picks up the drum, shakes off the dust, and beats it.

"Sounds pretty," he says and takes it with him.

Lum dreams that the *rehue* is in flames, set ablaze by gray crows carrying fire in their beaks. Members of the tribe rush to extinguish it, but an evil spirit prevents them from getting close to it. Young and old kneel around the burning totem in a circle, and the children cry. Suddenly, one of the crows grows larger and becomes a skinny mare that gallops away, dragging a corpse. Lum struggles to see its face to no avail and wakes up.

She opens her eyes and feels something brushing the straw that covers her. As she tries to come to her senses and shake off her dream, she sees blackbirds swirling around her head. She tries to shoo them away but is too weak and dizzy. She rolls over and vomits, then wipes her mouth with the palm of her hand, rises to her feet, unsteady and sore, and looks at the straw stuck to her freshly scraped skin.

Lum takes a sip of *chicha* from a pot, and still feverish, heads back to the village. She thinks that once she returns and shares the triumph of her journey of initiation, she'll be able to heal the sick and shepherd the dead. She'll become indispensable, and all the people who thought she was strange will finally accept her. She'll show them what she can do, and even though it may be a struggle, she believes she'll be successful. It's all a matter of time.

She walks slowly and spies an ostrich egg shining in the grasses. She goes over and picks it up, realizing as it crumbles between her fingers that it's as cracked as the arid land.

The soldiers have made a campfire and the lieutenant orders, "Carranza, go with Ancatril and butcher a mare for us to eat."

"Why do I have to go with that Indian?" asks the soldier.

Ancatril looks at the lieutenant letting him know he doesn't like Carranza's company either.

"I've heard enough. Rufino, help Ancatril butcher a mare so we can eat once and for all!"

Rufino and Ancatril lasso a mare and tie it to a tree. They bind its legs, and once they have it under control, pull it to the ground. Ancatril takes his knife and makes a deep slash in the belly where the arteries run. A stream of blood gushes out, and the mare neighs and twists to bite him. Rufino holds its head while the Indian ties a rope around its jaw. Ancatril presses the wound with his hands to speed the bleeding so the animal will die quicker.

After completing the tedious task of skinning and butchering the mare, they go to the well to wash up. Ancatril says they need to wait awhile to tenderize the meat, but Rufino rushes him. The Indian salts the pieces, sticks them in a pot of water, and boils them over the fire to make a stew, murmuring as he cuts the meat:

Oh!, chachai, vita uentru, reyne mapo, frenean votrey, fille, enteu, come que hiloto, come que ptoco, come que amaotu.

*Pavre laga inche, Hito to elaemy? Tefa quinie vusa hilo, hiloto tu fiñay.**

The men sit around the fire pit, gazing in silence at the flames as they eat, chewing, sucking up the grease and devouring the meat to the bone. Gorged, they stretch out and pick at the meat stuck between their teeth.

---

*Oh! Father, great man and king of this land, bless me, dear friend, every day, with good food, good water, and good sleep. I am poor. Are you hungry? Take this poor meal, eat if you wish.

Ancatril gets up to prepare *mate*. His mule waits for him, nodding its head, and he pats its rump, before untying a leather bag filled with water.

The animals drink from a pool, and the men quench their thirst as well. The sun's beating down, although off in the distance dark clouds appear on the horizon like a rope stretched out over the plain. Deus measures the land with long strides and sketches a plat in pencil.

Fields of thistle sway in the northern wind. The stench of burning bodies mixes with the smell of the stew. Bodies piled one on top of the other form walls, and featherless blackbirds peck between the spaces of a neck or a dangling arm. Embers crackle and the air becomes more and more dense. A reptile slithers from the tall grasses into the thickets.

Acting the hero, Rufino recounts:

"We were prepared, with rifles loaded as we waited to attack. The Indians had climbed the hill so they'd see us coming, but they found troops on horseback waiting for them in silence, without yet firing a shot. We stayed still, watching every move of those savages who threatened us from all sides as they advanced on foot. We had orders not to shoot until we could take them down. We let them approach until they were about fifty paces from us and then opened fire. Those on foot retreated and tried to hide among the scrubby *ñire* and *espinillo* trees. Those riding horses quickly set fire to the field, and the wind fed the flames in their favor, forcing us to change our position.

"The fire scorched the faces and bodies of some of our troops. The Indians took advantage of the situation to charge again with *boleadoras*, and we suffered casualties. I'll never forget one soldier who was hit in the head by one of those flying balls and died instantly, like he'd been struck by lightning. I remember that I grabbed my dagger in fury, caught one of them, and went for his heart. The savage looked at me without flinching, he was the leader. I didn't hesitate. I impaled him with the blade, and at that very moment reinforcement troops from the fort arrived and joined the battle. Like a hurricane of steel, we pursued and assaulted them with our sabers. Only a few were able to flee."

"A storm's coming. It's time to leave," says Ancatril.

The squadron heads west, leaving behind what's left of the village.

Three centennial calden trees survive the fire.

Lum lifts her head, sniffs, and smells something that turns her stomach. She looks at the sky and everything around her spins. She talks to herself, muttering incomprehensible words. She takes one step, then another, zigzagging until she comes to the edge of what used to be the village and is now just a field covered with a black crust. Lum walks among the ruins of the massacre, rubbing her eyes.

Ngenechen, are you the one who places these images before my eyes? Am I still dreaming?

She believes she recognizes some faces among the bodies and a short distance away catches sight of the *machi's* poncho. At first Lum stands still, then screams and runs over to her teacher, embracing her body and sobbing. She lies there for a long time, helpless. As she rests her face on the *machi's* cheek, she realizes there's something she must do, and rises.

I'm a machi now, and I must fulfill the ritual and guide the spirits of the dead. The cultrún . . .

Lum searches everywhere for the drum but it's nowhere to be seen. Devastated, she falls to her knees with her hands on the ground, her gaze lost in so much death. She fills her hands with ashes and rubs her face until it turns gray, just as the shamans do to take on the glow of the phantoms and become one of them.

Campaign Journal, May 25, 1879

We recently began the journey home. More than one hundred leagues separate us from our great city, Buenos Aires. We were victorious. The spoils of the battle included one hundred Indians, five hundred rescued animals, and also a dozen white women who had been held captive. The Remington rifle, or "Indian-killer," as the savages call it, is a veritable miracle of engineering. Thanks to it, we were able to conquer the village with few casualties and little effort. I believe it is possible to declare with certainty that the campaign to conquer the desert has been won.

We took the precaution to divide ourselves into three groups. The first left to secure the front line. The majority of the troops followed later with the rescued captives, prisoners, and animals. And our squad, a handful of men, are leaving now to bring up the rear. We should be arriving at the fort a few hours after the troops commanded by Lieutenant Sanabria.

The *Pampa* has been conquered. The General can rest easy.

Lt. Marcial Obligado

Lum hears galloping nearby and sees a mare running in circles, afraid of the smoke still rising from the burning huts. She clicks her tongue for the horse to come, and walks over to it slowly and caresses its back.

You have a powerful spirit and I'll have the courage to survive if I have you with me. I'm going to give you a sip of my chicha, so we'll both be strong.

Lum pours a drink from her leather sack into the mare's mouth, then mounts bareback, taking one last look at the burning village before leaving.

On the Journey

"How many leagues before we reach the fort?"

"We need to follow the Colorado River," Ancatril replies.

Deus checks his compass and confirms they're heading in the right direction. The tall grasses shimmer under the glaring sun, swaying as a cold wind sweeps across their plumes.

In the distance, the men see a figure swinging like a pendulum in a whirlwind of blue and bone-colored flecks of dust. They approach and see a hanged Indian, whose once proud countenance was reduced to a moronic smirk frozen in a final expression of defiance.

"He must have been hanging a long time before we got here," Rufino remarks, while the others pass by him in silence.

Perturbed, Sergeant Carranza rubs his neck, brings his horse to a halt, and stays there, saying in a low voice, "It was November or December . . ."

"What was?"

"I remember when the Indians attacked. That hanged Indian reminded me of that raid. As they got closer, you could hear reeds snapping in the marsh and their war cries and the sound of rattles made from hooves, seeds, bones, and animal teeth that they wore around their ankles. There were no footprints but they found me anyway.

"Before the raid, the Indians poisoned my dogs. They had spasms and couldn't walk. I couldn't take them with me or leave them behind, so I had to kill them. I ran and kept running over the slippery mud, with nowhere to hide. There was nothing but the moon and a mob of Indians. Fleeing shadows, I looked for a hiding place among the reeds and went deep into the grasslands. Ticks climbed my legs, and I thought I was going to die from pain while I waited for them to come and find me and slit my throat."

"Are you all right, Carranza?" asks Rufino. "Have a drink, the mob isn't going to come."

"They're not human, they're . . ." Carranza rambles.

The lieutenant gives the order to move on.

Puán Border, 1876

It's Sunday, and Ancatril is headed for a post on the border to barter the sack of ponchos he's carrying over his shoulder. When he arrives, he unloads the ponchos he's brought to exchange. A white man comes over and offers him a meter of fabric. Ancatril says one of his ponchos alone is worth more than that remnant. The man disagrees, grabs one of them, says it's poorly made, and throws it at him with disdain.

At that moment, a couple of soldiers wearing faded jackets with epaulets on the shoulders approach Ancatril and surround him. Before he realizes what's happening, they seize him by the arms and force him to walk, threatening him with the point of a bayonet. The Indian tries to get away, and they tell him to stop resisting and get moving. The white man who'd come to barter quickly gathers up the ponchos scattered on the ground.

They blindfold Ancatril, then force him to climb into a wagon holding other young Indians. The wagon makes a rapid departure, pulled by four horses, and the two white soldiers accompany the captives, threatening them at gunpoint. Their voices resound in Ancatril's ears, repeating the word, "trench."

The squadron travels past a hill, dry pastures, tall grasses and thorny bushes. As the sun sets behind the woods, Deus says, "Lieutenant, I'm going to capture the landscape."

They stop, and Deus and Ancatril unload the crate with the camera equipment from the mule and set it up. Deus removes his jacket, rolls up his sleeves, and cleans his hands with a handkerchief. Then he takes out the tripod, unfolds it and mounts the camera box.

"For the first time, a three-legged creature inhabits the desert," Deus declares.

Inside the crate are labeled sepia-colored bottles and a box for storing the wet plates. Deus coats one of them with a solution, inhaling the invisible vapors of the weightless ether. He peers through the glass lens and sees the *canelo* trees rising more than fifteen meters, their foliage shining like silver.

"The desert speaks," says Deus.

He can't capture the moment because only dust and light will appear. He needs the opaque mass of bodies to compose the image.

"Stand together so I can take a portrait of you," he tells them.

Rufino gets off his horse and goes over to the box.

"Can I touch it?"

"No, no you can't," responds the photographer.

"Don't move," says Deus as he ducks his head beneath the cloth. He presses the shutter release, sending a chill through Ancatril's body.

No one moves while the diaphragm closes. Then Deus unscrews the camera box, carries it over to the crate, and takes cover beneath a black cloth. Fluid runs over the tilted plates that can be heard sliding in and out. The photographer reappears with his face flushed, wearing the black cloth like a cape.

"We want to see ourselves," the lieutenant says.

It's past six o'clock. Rufino doesn't know how to tell time, but he takes the watch that belonged to Ordoñez out of his pocket. It's stopped, so he shakes it and holds it up to his ear, then puts it away.

"I want to smoke," he says.

The lieutenant throws him a pouch of tobacco.

"Roll a cigarette for each of us."

The paper rustles as the soldier's fingers roll the cigarettes, one after the other. The men inhale and blow out the smoke.

"Let's go, we've been here too long," says the lieutenant.

Ancatril stays with the animals while the others move ahead to find a place to spend the night. They carry packs and saddlebags on their backs as they go into the forest. The sky's turning gray, but the rain holds off.

The men forge ahead, crossing swampy terrain. Soaked in sweat, the horses pant and the clanking of their horseshoes is silenced as their hooves sink into the mud. They struggle to free themselves, and their spirits seem to lift when they reach solid ground. Voices echo in the void of the barren desert and from their hidden burrows the squealing of rats resounds.

The men set up camp at dusk in a grove of calden trees. Ancatril brings the animals and ties them to a trunk.

The lieutenant complains about the mosquitos.

"Indian, light a fire to keep these bugs from eating us alive."

"We're surrounded by trees, Lieutenant. It's not a good idea to light a fire here sir, where it hasn't rained for days. If we keep moving, we'll come to a lagoon about three leagues away."

"You're not going to tell me how to set up camp. You do what I tell you."

Ancatril obeys without hiding his concern. With dry branches everywhere, it takes no time for the men to make a fire. Ancatril looks around and says some prayers. Carranza makes fun of him and the Indian falls silent and leaves to fetch a pot.

A breeze is blowing and sparks fly, setting fire to a bush a meter away. Ancatril runs to put it out, but a second later another bush catches fire. Minutes later they're surrounded by a tower of flames. The men quickly gather what they can. Deus grabs his photography equipment and rushes away before the others have a chance to react. Carranza follows him, as do the rest when they realize it's futile to keep trying to extinguish the flames.

The men ride off in the opposite direction of the wind to escape the fire, leaving the woods behind. They come to a clearing and stop to catch their breath not far from the flames.

"We should keep moving," Ancatril says.

The lieutenant stares at him, fed up.

"You still haven't learned your place."

The Indian looks away, and the lieutenant gives the order to move on.

Alsina's Trench, 1876

One day some Indians from Puán arrive at the Sauce Seco Post, among them Ancatril. He doesn't know how to read or write, but he understands Spanish and interprets for the others what work they have to do and explains that they'll be given food and quarters.

The Indians are forced to sign with a cross at the bottom of a blank sheet of paper. They don blue wool uniforms, leather riding boots, and military caps, and are sent off to dig a trench under the hot sun. A scribe reads aloud the enlistment roll.

Dozens of eyes blink in the dim light, and the noise is deafening. Time is kept for those below by those who give orders above. On cold afternoons the wind blows so fiercely that it suffocates the diggers who try to stay warm by huddling together. They seem like those characters from an ancient tale who began a journey knowing it would be nearly impossible to return alive. At night, they still hear themselves digging, and in their dreams, that dank ominous pit near the center of the earth becomes a serpent that rises out of the darkness while they're sleeping and devours them, expelling flames and laying eggs in their blood. It stretches out over the plain until it can no longer be seen. When the men awaken from that nightmare, they don't know where they are, but they have to return to the trench. Some are so stiff and parched they can't stand and finally give up, taking their final breath as they burrow through the tunnel. Poisoned by dysentery or typhus, some collapse, swallowing dirt, and are immediately buried.

That morning it rains so hard the trench begins to flood, and as the men dig and shovel, mud covers them from head to toe. They try to climb over each other to escape that hole, and like ants crawling to the light, the men emerge blinded, their arms heavy as iron bars. The strongest don't sink in the mud and keep carrying buckets of clay to reinforce the wall. The water cracks the walls, and they crumble. Mud cascades in torrents about six or seven meters high.

"The wall's going to collapse," they cry from above.

Ancatril struggles as rushing water strikes his back, forcing him to bend over. Tons of dirt crash with a roar, and suddenly it becomes pitch black.

It was the lieutenant who gave the order to dig him out. The lad had shown he was strong even though a heap of earth had covered him. Once they got him to the surface, they poured water over him. He'd been blind for a day and a half. The lieutenant has never forgotten the look on the Indian's face, covered in that thick black liquid, blinking as he chewed a piece of bread they'd given him to calm down.

After distinguishing himself in battle, the lieutenant received his commission and was assigned another private for his troop, and so he chose Ancatril after seeing his courage and because he spoke Spanish well and wasn't afraid to speak his mind. The Indian was always of service to him and thanked him more than once for not leaving him buried in the trench.

The lieutenant hangs onto the branch of a tree, breathless. He closes his eyes and sees patches of brightness flickering on and off in the darkness as the lighthouse casts an intermittent glow over the surface of the sea. He hears the wind howling and the whistle of a passing boat, but he doesn't move, and it feels as if the dock is moving closer. The lieutenant is a boy who plays kick the can with Hueñi. His Indian grandfather comes looking for them at night, walking with the lilting sway of an ox as he calls them. It begins to rain and they run down the street, and his father opens the door and embraces him.

The lieutenant wishes his dead father could be with him. He's alone, just as he was when he finished school. And he was alone at the graduation party, where chandeliers illuminated the cold hallways.

"Congratulations, my friend," an Indian boy standing at the entrance told him. It was Hueñi, but the lieutenant couldn't bring himself to stop and greet him. He rushed down the staircase, grasping the banister that was as smooth as the wood of the Patagonian calden trees.

[

The Calden Trees. *Viaje al país de los araucanos.*
Estanislao S. Zevallos, Biblioteca Dimensión.
Buenos Aires, Ediciones Solar, 1994, p. 191.

Since leaving the place where her village once stood, Lum has been restless, constantly looking over her shoulder, possessed by a thought that haunts her. The eye of the desert is watching her. When her hands tremble, she entwines her fingers into the horse's mane and holds on tightly, hoping to gain a sense of security.

A few kilometers from the woods, Lum sees a dwindling fire. The smoke casts a shadow on the horizon, and as the young *machi* rides toward the fire, a thick cloud shrouds the afternoon in emptiness. She and her mare vanish amidst the black skeletons of the calden trees.

Death

In the Eye of the Sea Lagoon

As night falls, the men reach the lagoon, exhausted after escaping the blazing forest of calden trees. Ancatril takes off his boots and leads his horse by the bridle, walking barefoot over ground still warm from the sun. Light pink water washes up on the shore of the deep lagoon, forming a crust of sea salt that shimmers among the grasses, nettles, and devil's claw. He steps into the cold water and washes his neck and face but doesn't drink because it's salty. He's never seen the sea, but someone once told him about the white foam that clings to the shore when the water recedes.

Another lagoon appears on the still surface, a secluded mirage reflecting the quivering branches of young acacia trees. Blue-gray sand dunes loom in the distance, and smoke rises from a mound of corpses, a common sight in the desert. The wind howls as a family of *guanacos* run from a puma, then vanish into a hollow. They say animals and humans can die from shock in this land.

The horses quench their thirst and graze on buds they find among the thistle, at ease while they chomp at the bit and paw the ground. Deus stares at his compass, baffled by the arrow spinning round and round. The lieutenant's face is etched with fatigue and his wrinkles seem even deeper under the radiance cast by the lagoon.

He says to Deus, sitting next to him, "Do you know how the war started, Deus? It was over cattle and fear that the Indians would come and kill you, slaughter you even if you hadn't killed a soul. That's how we became more patriotic. We got ready for battle with horses and weapons. That's the real reason we left our homes to come to this godforsaken place. There's no glory Deus, going to war is worse than raising pigs."

"You're saying we're driven by our own fears of the Indians, and we carry those murderers inside us."

The lieutenant clears his dry mouth and spits out phlegm.

"You have a swig?"

"No, Lieutenant, there's nothing left after that disaster. I only thought about saving my equipment, I'm sorry. Maybe that savage has some left."

"Ask him to bring me some rum."

Deus orders the Indian to bring the flask. Ancatril hurries to fetch it from the saddlebag and then hands it to the lieutenant, who takes a gulp.

The photographer sits on his saddle with his fingers intertwined, so close to the lieutenant their arms brush each other. The lieutenant's dark eyes evoke war, lost time, exile. The suffering they reveal is much deeper than any abyss over which Deus has ever peered.

"I don't think the raiders will ever surrender, Lieutenant. The savages rule the desert."

"Maybe so."

The lieutenant picks up the *cultrún* and examines it carefully, running his rough had over the drawings.

"Those Indians did a fine job."

The lieutenant strikes it, trying to understand something.

Carranza has served twenty years on the front. He's suffered from insomnia for a long time, often lying awake to avoid those troubling visions that torment him more and more frequently.

This evening the soldier leaves his horse nearby and leans back on a large rock, settling down and finally falling asleep with his body slumped over, his head bowed, and a pistol in his hand. Minutes later, the sound of footsteps startle him and he rises quickly, grabs the enemy by the hair, and sticks the barrel of the gun down his throat.

"Let go, it's me!" Ancatril manages to shout.

Carranza recognizes him, and puts his pistol back in the holster. The sun is sinking, and the horses, asleep on their feet, seem like serene giants contemplating the heart of the desert.

"The raiders . . . are they all dead?" Carranza asks.

"Yes," replies the Indian.

Carranza breathes a sigh of relief. Ancatril doesn't know what to say and improvises.

"You were loyal, Sergeant. You always took care of your people."

Carranza takes out his weapon again, adjusts his cap, and stands at attention. Then they walk side by side back to the campfire.

Deus sees Ancatril standing next to Carranza about fifty meters away, their backs turned and the lagoon in the background. The photographer gauges the intensity of the light on their gray bodies. He thinks he hears the diaphragm closing, but his retina can't focus on the image in that blinding glare.

Barefoot, without his jacket and his pants rolled up, Carranza sticks his feet in the water.

"I'm going to take a quick dip," he says.

"Don't go too far out, Sergeant," Ancatril advises him. "They say whirlpools appear in this lagoon sometimes, and the water can suck you in. Even if you swim fast, the current will drag you down and swallow you."

"I'm not afraid of the water," Carranza replies, walking away, along the shore, holding his cap and splashing his feet in water frothy as egg whites.

When he can no longer hear the voices in the distance, Sergeant Carranza calms down, stopping when he comes to a bend to rest, as if the world had always been a pleasant place to inhabit.

Lum reaches the other side of the lagoon where she discovers the men's campsite.

They shouldn't see me.

She dismounts and ties her mare to a tree. Crouching, she walks silently along the edge of the lagoon. When she gets halfway between the men and her mare, she stops and watches them. Then she hears a sound that makes her heart beat faster. She raises her head to determine where the sound's coming from, and when she sees the lieutenant clumsily playing the *cultrún*, her eyes fill with rage.

Ngenechen, give me strength. I have no village and no family, only this mare you've given me and the land that nourishes me. There's no reason for me to be in this world now that they've taken everything away from me, Ngenechen. Those were the huincas, *the white men brought by the* gualicho. *And my mother told me that we must fear the* gualicho, *the evil spirit that's everywhere. It's a disease, a disaster, it lives in the foul water of this lagoon, and the* gualicho *has found its way inside me.*

With her right hand, Lum grabs the knife she keeps at her waist and crawls to the water.

The lieutenant steps back, dazzled by the light reflected in the mirror of water, and glimpses an outline of a dark figure that vanishes, swallowed up by the lagoon.

Carranza urinates, discharging a warm stream from side to side until it dwindles to nothing. Then he sits down and contemplates the landscape. During this long journey, he's never seen so much water and sand in the same place. He struggles to his feet, then goes into the lagoon and swims, turning his head with each stroke, counting to seventy before swimming back to where he can stand up. He swallows his saliva and blows out to try to get rid of the sharp noise in his head, but his ears are still plugged. Then he lies face up, floating and gazing serenely at the passing clouds. Without a breeze, the puffs of red clouds barely move, hovering in a hazy stillness, and he can't tell if the lagoon is gray and the sky pink or the opposite. He turns his head toward the shore, moving further away from the sand until it disappears from sight. Dozing, his body drifts away like a floating stick.

Lum lets the water embrace her, then dives under and swims. She must do what she's decided and ignore the thoughts tormenting her. She stays afloat holding onto some roots, while the enveloping womb of the lagoon soothes her.

Lum takes slow strokes, holding her breath. She sees the silhouette of a man floating above her head and advances like a predator from the depths until she's right under his back. Then she tugs at Carranza's pants, clasps her legs around his waist, gripping him, and thrusts the knife into him, stabbing him over and over between his ribs. His screams are silenced beneath the water. He struggles to free himself from those legs, but can't get loose, and finally his body goes limp, and he stops breathing.

The fury inside Lum slowly abates, and a surge of strange emotions comes over her as she watches the blood flow. She looks at the floating corpse with indifference even though she was the one who killed him.

The lieutenant calls out to Carranza. With no moon, the night is pitch-black and the light from the campfire barely illuminates the area near the men.

"Did anyone see Carranza?" he asks.

Upon hearing the negative response from his men, the lieutenant becomes worried.

"Knowing him, he could have drowned."

When Rufino chuckles, the lieutenant commands, "This is no laughing matter. Search for him!"

Deus, Rufino, and Ancatril carry torches and walk a short distance into the lagoon to cast the light as they call out for Carranza.

"You can't see a thing, Lieutenant!" Deus shouts.

"Pardon me, sir, but until the sun rises, it's useless to look for him," says the Indian.

"If Carranza's alive, he'll know how to return. Let's all get some sleep," the lieutenant grumbles.

The men return with relief. No one cares to search for someone lost in the darkness of that lagoon.

Lum swims, pushing the corpse, until she reaches the shore opposite the campsite. She takes a rope out of her satchel and looks for a heavy rock. She finds one and manages to carry it over to the dead man and tie it to his legs. Her muscles twitch and her teeth chatter, and suddenly everything turns white and she nearly faints. She sits down for a moment and breathes deeply until she recovers.

Carranza's cadaver has an open mouth, as if he were shouting, and the young *machi* doesn't want to look at him. Lum drags the body back into the lagoon, diving underwater and submerging him as deeply as she can.

The lieutenant was the only one who didn't sleep a wink. Carranza's disappearance left him anxious.

As soon as dawn breaks, he awakens his men to begin the search.

"If he'd drowned, we'd see him floating," Deus concludes.

"That lousy coward's a deserter," Rufino remarks.

The lieutenant focuses on the shoreline with apprehension and commands, "Go all the way around the lagoon, and find some sign of him."

Rufino and the Indian head to the left, and the lieutenant and Deus go to the right. A half-hour later they meet on the other side.

"Nothing, Lieutenant," Rufino reports.

Everyone remains silent, until Ancatril exclaims:

"The lagoon swallowed him up!"

"Don't be superstitious," Deus tells him.

"Enough," the lieutenant sighs.

"This is bullshit," Rufino protests.

The others look at each other and no one knows what to say.

The lieutenant is the first to get them on their way.

"We have to move on and get to the fort. If Carranza deserted, we'll report him, and if he died, he's better off."

There's a look of uncertainty and unease in their eyes.

As the horses gallop against the wind, their hooves pound rhythmically like a scythe shearing everything in its way, leaving furrows in the trampled ground.

Not far away the outline of an acacia tree with its five-pointed blossoms graces the horizon. Rising a meter and a half over a sandbank, stands a cactus whose stalk is as green as wetland vines because of the water stored inside. It's adorned by a flower with white stamens and purple veins converging in the center.

Lum follows the four men, keeping them in sight from a safe distance. She's figured out who's in command and also saw that an Indian is part of the group. All alone, her resolve seems futile, and she wonders why she's taken on this mission when she could go far away with her mare. She places her ear on its neck and listens to its heart beating in unison with hers.

I had to do it, Ngenechen. It was a sacrifice, she whispers.

As she gallops, she passes enormous trees, the oldest living beings. They fill her with respect and remind her of the elder members of her tribe. She carries nothing more than a satchel and a leather hide to cover herself. She barely has any food, only a few biscuits and a pouch of fresh water, and only her mare for company.

A puma drags a *guanaco* by the nape of the neck and tears the flesh of its prey, breaking the silence of the Eye of the Sea Lagoon with the sound of teeth crushing cartilage.

Mileposts

Deus sets up the theodolite, rotating it on its tripod as he records measurements on a topographical map. He determines the highest point of the terrain, notes the coordinates and marks the map with a cross. Then he drives a stake into the ground to indicate where the army has passed on its march through the desert and the spot where the boundary marker will be erected.

"This land will be worth a fortune once it's fenced in," Deus exclaims.

"Rufino, did you know that more than thirty years have passed since the first ranch was fenced in with barbed wire?"

The soldier shakes his head no, not interested in the least.

"It was in 1845, I believe, when they brought the barbed wire from England. Now it's a widely-used method in the rural areas that lends order to this country hounded by barbarians. The most progressive ranch owners erected barbed-wire fences before they planted thorny *espino* shrubs or placed boundary markers. The transformation of the *pampas* will be slow, but that's how the cattle industry and foreign investment will grow more rapidly, and the country will develop.

"Nothing's wasted if it's fenced in. It's a necessary investment," proclaims the photographer.

"These Indians never knew how to manage the land or profit from it," he adds.

Rufino rakes the sand with his feet like a chicken. He feels the blast of the red wind moving through the trees, joining forces around that circle of sand.

"Look, Deus, there are tracks here," Rufino says, but Deus pays him no mind as he draws a figure with his raised hand and notes details about the location in his sketchbook.

"My, how well we eat in the desert," says Rufino as he saunters, exposing his pot belly under his unbuttoned shirt when he bends backward. He whistles as he heads into the trees, the grass rustling under each step he takes. He sings with pride as he urinates, *Oh, we swear to die with glory.*

"Rufino, stop fooling around and get to work," the lieutenant orders.

At the spot calculated by Deus, Rufino and the Indian must pile large stones to mark the conquered land. Reluctantly, Rufino searches for rocks, knowing they should be somewhat flat. He finds one and carries it, dragging his feet and leaving a trail like a plow. He steps in a puddle and slips but catches his balance, thinking:

If I get out of this, I'm never going to get my hands dirty again.

He drops a stone, huffs and puffs, and wipes his forehead with a sleeve, saying to himself without speaking out loud:

Stack them up, dig a grave. Since they enlisted me, I've buried so many traitors, I'm long overdue for a promotion.

"We built the marker, Lieutenant," says Ancatril.

The soldiers have dark circles under their eyes. Rufino tears away a bit of a crushed fingernail and Deus brushes dirt off his pants.

The marker looks sturdy although it leans a bit.

"You made it crooked," Rufino says to Ancatril.

"What's that over there?" Deus asks.

"Bones," Rufino responds.

A green light outlines the dunes.

"Do you remember that time we went to the slaughterhouse to buy meat?" Deus asks.

"Yes, I remember it like it was yesterday. It was swarming with flies and stunk of rotten meat and dead animals. One of the workers had a face covered with erysipelas and fever made him sweat as he butchered the meat."

The photographer feels overwhelmed and filthy again, just remembering how easy it was to contract a disease in the slaughterhouse. Deus wanted to get out of that place as quickly as possible and scrub himself with soap.

Lum circles round and round the soldiers on her mare, keeping her distance as she tries to find a way to approach them. It was easy to clear her tracks at the lagoon; now she'd have to be more clever, taking precautions with every move. She trembles from the cold and yearns for the warmth of a fire, but knows full well she can't let them see smoke and give herself away. She's familiar with the area and heads for a nearby cave.

Once she finds it, she dismounts and gathers branches. Then she enters a kind of den, and though she never feared darkness before, she does now, perhaps because before she'd always had her mother or the *machi* by her side.

Lum rubs two stones together and sparks fly. She adds dry leaves, and as the flame begins to burn, she stays close by, gazing at it. There's a flash of white light, and she remembers when she used to help her mother make clay pots.

She peers into the cave and sees a dead condor. She digs a hole with her hands, picks it up, and as she buries it, remembers how her mother used to tell her that when you bury a bird, it will be reborn.

She's tormented by spirits that want revenge and feels like a vulnerable and useless *machi* without the *cultrún*. Lum knows those soldiers can close in on her and everything will end terribly. She feels something gripping and crushing her heart. Silence hovers like a bitter fruit and Lum thinks:

Only the dead accompany me.

Lum believes that for the people of the desert, this is a land that will never perish. A mountain is a mountain and a river a river. You can climb to the left or the right, glide through fields of thistle, and you arrive home again.

Tormented by insomnia, Lum lies deep inside the cave, listening to the beats of her heart. She believes whatever is desired will come at the right time to those who are prepared, and yet she is bombarded by thoughts. She feels as if an abyss is opening under her feet, and layers of fog are bearing down on her.

Perhaps it's nothing more than the light and the warmth of the flames that awaken her, like a sprout waiting for the perfect time to open. The *machi* taught her such secrets:

If logs are arranged as they should be, the fire will ignite on its own.

Lum gets up slowly, snaps her fingers, and begins to feel the force of the earth penetrating deep inside her. She needs everything to be in its rightful place again, and thinks:

Horses don't fly; water doesn't overflow the river; the stars, unlike men, don't clash with each other.

Lum evokes the name of the old *machi* out loud. The cave sends it back in an echo, and she no longer feels so alone. She leaves the refuge and mounts her mare. The moon looms above like a watchful eye as a shiver runs up and down her spine when she believes she sees Carranza's wide-open gray eyes once again.

"*Choique*," shouts Ancatril, and his voice resounds on the plain.

He digs in his spurs to speed his horse on and raises his arm in the air, swinging the *boleadora* as he rides. A feathered cloud crosses their path about two hundred meters away. The horse neighs, and man and animal are one as they descend the gully. A shadow slips between the tall rippling grasses, wavers, and streams onto the dunes. Time quickens, slipping through the fingers. The Indian hurls the *bolas*, hits the target, and collects his prey.

The ostrich hangs with its beak open and its feathers still moving until it's finally stuffed into a burlap sack. The Indian sprinkles a few fistfuls of salt over it, loads it onto the mule, and the squadron of soldiers resume their march.

Ancatril untied the sack hanging from the saddle, removed the ostrich and cut a few slashes below its thighs, tugging the skin all the way to the head and making a raspy sound. He cut the neck and threw away the feather-covered hide, then lit a fire while the others set up camp.

A light mist turns the dust to ice, hovers in the air, and settles over the treetops. The men roll cigarettes and smoke, sitting around the slow-burning fire. They throw down copper coins and bet on cards that snap from their hands. Each are dealt three cards, and they rearrange them between their fingers. Not even a fly stirs as they plan their strategies.

"Did you see that? Rufino asks.

"What?" asks Deus.

"Maybe it was a hare."

"What happened?" Deus insists.

"I thought I saw something moving over there, behind those trees."

"Today I was thinking that I barely remember Carranza," Rufino said.

"Some things we just don't remember, as if they never happened," says the lieutenant.

"Yes, as if they were ghosts," Deus adds.

The lieutenant considers the four of clubs in his hand.

"What are we betting for?" Deus asks.

"For money, what else?" Rufino remarks.

"Money means nothing in the *pampa*. Whoever wants to earn a fortune needs to conquer land. That's what the general said, and that's why we're here," retorts Deus.

Juice drips off the meat and slips over the coals, emitting a puff of salty smoke that makes their mouths water.

"Did you turn the ostrich over, soldier?" asks the lieutenant.

Ancatril gets up to stir the coals with a long stick.

Rufino rubs his palms together. Ordoñez's pocket watch is still safe inside the lining of his jacket.

"You want to play that card now, Lieutenant?"

"Don't rush me, the war's over."

"There'll be another one," replies the soldier.

The lieutenant seems lost in thought.

"I hope there'll still be work for us," Rufino adds.

"We're hungry," says Deus. "How much longer?"

"A while," responds the Indian.

The lieutenant waits before playing his card, takes a puff, and then chooses another card before saying with indifference, "I pass."

"This damn jack's killing me," says Rufino and throws down a seven of spades.

The forest conceals the horizon, but a small patch of gloomy sky peeks through a clearing.

Rufino spies a lizard crawling near Deus, grabs it slyly and sticks it down the photographer's shirt. Deus jumps up and screams, shaking his shirt, but can't get rid of the creature. Rufino laughs, holding his belly. The lieutenant and Ancatril join in the laughter.

Deus finally gets rid of the lizard and kicks at Rufino, who is fast enough to grasp the photographer's foot in mid-air and, still laughing, makes him fall to the ground. Deus's face is red with rage and he tangles on the ground with Rufino, who quickly gets the better of him, putting him in a hold.

"You give up, Deus? Come on, don't be mad, take a photograph of us."

Rufino lets go of him and cackles loudly again.

Deus has no option but to surrender, lessening the tension as he joins them. They all laugh a bit, and slowly the laughter abides and the uneasiness returns more intense than before.

Rufino sighs and looks down at the meat Ancatril has just served him. The others, seated in silence, take advantage of the food being served to restore distance between themselves.

As the sun sets over the plateau, Lum contemplates the desert stretched out below her like a long snake slithering through the dust. Her makeshift camp consists of a sheep hide and reeds, but no fire. Her mare grazes a few meters away, and she's eaten a few pieces of fruit.

Gazing at plants consoles and unites her with everything she misses. It'll be a long time before she's at peace again. A hollow sound stirs her thoughts:

An Indian is nothing without animals and grasses. How good it is to feel the earth beneath the soles of the feet.

A hare approaches Lum furtively, and the two look at each other. Winter's coming and the hare's tired of digging and digging only to find a few dried out tubers. It chews them as if it lives in a universe where time passes more swiftly.

Lum looks for something in her satchel and pulls out a small well-worn book that a captive named Ofelia had given her. She taught Lum and her mother to read, and when she holds the book in her hand, images of those moments spent slowly spelling words come back to her. She could never give up that book.

She takes a long time deciphering what it says. Each time she reads, she thinks about something that could have happened but no longer can. The desert seems like that book, each letter inscribed with a dip of blue ink, something mysterious scrawled over a background of vast darkness.

Lying on the ground, Lum turns the page to a paragraph that someone, perhaps Ofelia, had marked. Soon after Ofelia was brought to the village, the chief made her his wife. The kidnapped woman admired how he mounted his bay horse, but Lum never could understand what attracted her to a chief who was so much older than she. Lum closes the book and lies there quietly thinking how different Ofelia was from the other whites. It seems so strange to her, so hard to understand.

Something builds up in Lum that she can barely control. She stands up and begins to pace from side to side, following an imaginary line as she speaks to herself:

Deceive them, trap them, corner them, at night . . . how can I get close to those men without them seeing me?

A plan comes to mind and her eyes turn bright. Lum walks away from the campsite. Rage sets her in motion, and she needs to move on, take the first step, then another, relying on her accomplices, the whistling wind and her mare, to transport her.

Not too far away, three vultures circle above. Large blue bottle flies compete to suck the liquid oozing out of the brains of an outlaw lying on a dune with his head smashed. A spear pierces the bone of his right thigh. The stench of rotten flesh fills the air, and before long a skeleton will be all that's left of him.

The wind carries away the bandit's hat.

Rufino hides behind a tree. He loads his Remington and runs his fingers down the barrel of the gun as he waits for his prey. Before shooting, he says to himself:

What the hell am I doing here? Who will remember us one hundred years from now?
Rufino shoots and a bird falls to the ground, fatally wounded.

From the tree where she's perched, Lum watches the soldier shoot a crow, and pain rushes through her body as if she'd been wounded as well.

That white man's a coward. I don't like his face.

The young *machi* believes that soldier has a hollow perverted soul and that life means nothing to him.

It's best he not find me.

Lum's legs are cramped from the cold, and she grows more and more weary as she tries to stay awake. She wishes the sun would rise and she could sleep for a long time.

Behind the foliage, a spark lights up like a firefly. The lieutenant adjusts his jacket. The medals of Coronel Ordóñez shine on its lapel. He takes a final puff of his cigarette before putting it out.

"We leave tomorrow, before dawn breaks," he says.

When the men turn in for the night, a sliver of light illuminates their silhouettes, stretched out like shipwrecked sailors floating on an icy sea. Silence falls over the camp.

Ancatril wraps himself in his blanket while he keeps watch. The lieutenant's words resound in his head:

"Soldier, don't fall asleep!"

A skunk sniffs around the campfire and finds bits of fat coated in sand. It grasps one in its paws, brushes it off, and savors it as it locks eyes with the Indian and keeps eating.

There are barely any Indians left to light fires in Patagonia, and nearly everything in the *pampa* has been wiped out.

It's hard for Ancatril to stay awake. He doesn't bother to put on the kettle. The *mate* leaves are wet, and the coals are just white lumps.

A storm's brewing to the west, with clouds as dark as ink covering the horizon and thunder rumbling in the distance. It hasn't rained for a long time.

"That storm will hit us tomorrow," says the Indian.

He doesn't want to move or make a sound. The lieutenant's orders were clear: *Keep your eyes open.*

Ancatril holds the icy weapon on his chest, trying to stay alert, but his head bobs and fatigue gets the best of him.

An owl perches on a bare branch of a calden tree, the moon over its head shining on its thick feathers. Rufino lies face up, unable to sleep, staring at it. Ancatril sleeps curled up in a ball with the pistol between his legs. He shivers, wakes up confused, and exclaims:

"Something terrible's coming."

"Stop making things up, Indian," Rufino scolds him.

"Listen, Rufino, I had a dream about this journey. I saw troops, an entire division disappearing among the dunes, and then the woods swallowed them alive."

"Stop screwing around, Indian, and sleep."

Ancatril turns on his left side, curls up again, but is now wide awake.

After gathering several fistfuls of *cebil* seeds, the same kind the *machi* gave her during her ceremony of initiation, Lum grinds them carefully in a makeshift mortar so that nothing goes to waste. The *machi* taught her how to make a powder called *paricá*, used to enter into a trance and communicate with the spirits.

So now they'll see the demon, and that gualicho *will take them away*, she whispers.

When she's ground all the *cebil* powder she needs, she puts it in her satchel and waits for everyone in the camp to fall asleep so that she can approach. Lum sneaks over to where the men keep the provisions, finds the coffee, and mixes it with the *cebil* powder, stirring it slowly with her hand.

Rufino talks in his sleep, mumbling nonsense. Startled, the young *machi* begins to retreat slowly without turning her back on the sleeping men, keeping her eye on Rufino, who grumbles in his slumber.

She finds shelter in the bushes, takes a deep breath, and lies down on the ground, breathing hard. Her shirt is filthy, and the skin scraped by the *machi* has turned purple where the scabs have dried up. They itch sometimes, and drops of blood appear where she scratched them. After lying there face down, she drags herself into the woods and disappears.

Illusions

The ground rumbles, and the vibrations pierce the eardrums. Something's approaching at lightning speed, breaking through at a full gallop; horseshoes shatter the ground, stirring up so much dust the foliage in the woods seems to vanish. The noise stops abruptly, and at that moment a horse with a midnight blue coat appears with his rider, a bloody soldier who can barely stay in his saddle. The sight of him makes the men's blood run cold. He's neither alive nor dead, but smells like charred jerky. Black foam oozes from a wound below his navel, and his legs shake uncontrollably. The right hand is missing the index finger and clutches a Remington to his chest. The soldier struggles to breathe. His arm is bandaged with strips of fabric tied with wire, and in the other hand he holds a knife like a centaur brandishing a sword. Over his sleeve he wears a faded armband. His skin is like leather. A thick liquid flows from his ears. He lifts his shoulder to support his head, looking at them with only one eye because the other's hanging by a nerve, and says:

"I was told to deliver this to your hands, Lieutenant. It was the final wish of a fallen soldier."

The lieutenant reaches out and accepts the knife, still aiming a pistol at him. The knife feels damp and warm and has a maroon-colored stone imbedded in its silver handle. The blade is sharp, and when the lieutenant cleans it on his pant leg, he reads the initials J. R. M.

"Everyone's dead. Don't go that way," says the blood-stained soldier.

"The sun's coming up. I'd best be on my way."

The soldier turns his horse around and heads into the brushwood; the pounding hooves echo in the air.

The campfire is dwindling, and dense smoke rises and fills the clearing.

"Long live the Desert of the South heroes!" shouts the soldier before he vanishes.

The lieutenant holsters the knife under his belt.

It's mid-morning, and Rufino has the feeling someone's following them. He goes over to the trees, and a sweet breeze entices him with the scent of a woman. Although he sees no one, he heads into the forest, straying from the campsite with the urge to find that phantom woman. But it's easy to get confused in the woods. Sometimes one ends up returning to the point of departure thinking he's traveled a long way, or he arrives somewhere he never intended to go.

The plain begins at the edge of the forest. Along the stream, the ground is so soft it's easy to lose one's footing in the muddy ravine. Further on, where the desert begins and sand dunes are shaped by the wind, the trails become blurred, disorienting the traveler.

The branches of the calden trees intertwine, and vines creep over them, forming inviting arches to pass through. Rufino struggles to make his way through the thicket. The vegetation hides him from sight and conceals his trail.

A piece of blue fabric clings to the thorns of the bramble.

General Store, 1861

Old James Barnes isn't afraid of Indians. He sells them liquor and tools in exchange for lassos, hides, and textiles he can offer at a high price. He keeps track of transactions in a book with a green cover and lets his customers buy on credit.

Barnes holds a stack of brown paper in his hand. He writes down a list of items that need to be repaired, then puts the pencil behind his ear. The scent of hay fills the store. He doesn't hear when the young boy Rufino comes in to ask for work.

"Afternoon. Do you want me to paint the front?"

Rufino's eyes are dark and shiny.

"What else do you know how to do, boy?"

"Whatever you like, sir."

The look on Rufino's face makes Barnes' heart stir. The old man takes a cup from the cupboard and places it in front of the boy. He dips a long-handled ladle into a milk can and fills the cup to the brim. Then he gives him bread and a knife.

"Sit down and eat," he tells him.

A block of cheese with a chunk missing sits in the middle of the counter. Rufino gulps down the milk, and Barnes fills his cup a second time. After that, the boy feels stronger.

Barnes gives him a bucket, brush, and ladder.

"You need to paint inside and out," he tells him.

Rufino prepares a mixture with one part bull's blood, one part lime, and one part water.

It's late, the store smells like paint, and its walls are rose-colored now. Under the lamplight, a bar of soap looks like a gold brick. Rufino wipes a rag over a shelf to get the dust off the dishes. A man with a sad look on his face is seated at the counter. Barnes serves him a glass of wine, and when he drinks it, his face breaks out in a red flush.

A moth flutters about and scales the wall. Rufino points at it with his index finger, holding one hand with the other, then enthusiastically shoots a blast of imaginary bullets. Giddy from the glow of the lamp, the moth crashes against the glass. Specks of dust fall from its wings, and a velvety spot of grease smudges the pane.

"Be still, boy," says Barnes in a hoarse voice.

Rufino stretches out on the feed bags. The man drinking wine asks him to sing a tune and the boy sings a folksong. His voice falls silent when a calvaryman enters, making the strands of the macraméed curtain sway. The tilted brim of his hat conceals his face. He wears an alpaca scarf over his shoulders, army pants, and bronze spurs. He walks over pounding his heels, each movement resounding like a whiplash. He sniffs the air and nods his head as a greeting. He stands near the man drinking wine and puts his elbows on the counter, then removes a tin can from his shirt pocket and offers cigarettes, revealing a silver ring on his middle finger. Barnes accepts one and lights it. The man drinking wine doesn't smoke but offers a gesture of appreciation.

"Virginia Tobacco," says old Barnes with pleasure.

The soldier asks for a light, and the old man hands him his cigarette. A column of smoke fills the corner where the men converse or say nothing. Rufino can't remember that.

"They told me you're from Europe," says the rider.

"That's right," Barnes answers.

The soldier flicks his ashes on the floor and asks,

"Where are you from?"

"England."

"I heard you like Indians."

"The *Mapuches* make good hides," Barnes replies.

"I don't deal with them. I prefer to do business with you. How much do you want for that lasso?"

Barnes takes it off the hook and hands it to him. "It costs one *peso.*"

The calvaryman yanks on the lasso and ties a knot. "A *peso* seems like a lot, Mister. How much could it have cost you?"

"That's the price I gave it. You don't have to buy it."

"You're making things difficult for me, Mister."

"It could cost more, sir."

The soldier raises the brim of his hat, and as the light hits his face, the two of them continue to bargain.

"Is that your final offer, Mister? It's a lot of money for something made by a savage."

"We're not going to fight over this. If you want it, give me eighty *centavos.*"

The soldier puts a one-*peso* coin on the table and waits for the change.

The man drinking wine asks what time it is, and the soldier takes out a gold watch from under his scarf.

"It's almost nine."

Rufino's never seen gold.

The man gulps the last drop of wine and gets out of his chair, leaving a *centavo* next to his glass.

"Where's the toilet?" he asks before rushing through the door holding his belly. His knife hits the floor with a thud.

"Turn right," Barnes tells him.

The strands of the macraméed curtain sway after the man goes through the doorway.

The soldier goes over and picks up the knife the man dropped, and Rufino watches him stash it under his waistband.

"Look, boy, that man who just left was a Federalist," says the soldier, as he looks outside, listening to the sound of the man's footsteps as he walks away.

He turns and says to Rufino:

"Never forget, a Federalist is a chickenshit who acts like a commander."

Barnes interrupts, "Come on sir, stop pestering the boy. How long will this feud between you last?"

"You have no business getting in the middle of this, being a foreigner, Mister."

"Stop fucking around," is what Barnes wanted to shout at the Unitarian, but a coughing fit contorted his face and kept him from speaking. When he recovered, he said, "From what I gather, you're not from around here either."

"I'm from Buenos Aires, Mister. Why don't you tell me what an Englishman is doing in the middle of the *pampa*."

Barnes remains silent and the Unitarian asks, "You like grilled meat, Mister?"

"Oh yes, the best part, the organs!" he says, nodding his head.

"We give those guts to the dogs."

Barnes laughs. "Do you want something to drink?"

"Nothing, Mister, just some water, if you don't mind."

The soldier keeps his head bowed, avoiding the old man's gaze. A scruffy beard can be seen below the brim of his hat. Barnes hooks his fingers under his suspenders and observes the stranger. The one-*peso* coin lies in the same spot.

"I'm not going to buy this," says the soldier as he returns the lasso.

"You're a tough customer," says the old man.

The soldier puts his money away.

"The thing is I don't like Redcoats."

"You're mistaken, friend, I never fought in the Army."

"There's nothing worse than a traitor."

"I don't regret escaping the war. This is a noble country. I came here so I wouldn't have to fight in Africa."

The soldier smells like the sweat of horses and the resin that Indians burn in winter. The gold watch hangs from his waist.

"Do you need anything, boss?" Rufino asks.

"No," says Barnes, and his expression loses its harsh edge.

The soldier grabs a chair, sits down, and crosses his legs.

"The war isn't going to end, Mister," he says, as he leans back and sharpens his knife, scraping the blade over his spur.

The Saltbed

Rufino wanders like a sleepwalker over a path covered in small crystals that sparkle beneath his sore feet. The silvery trees of the forest are now few and far between, and the scent of a woman no longer lingers in the air, lost without a trace. Seeds from broom shrubs cling to the cuffs of his pants. A briny taste fills his mouth as he meanders over what was once an ancient, desolate ocean, where fertile earth has been buried under layers of fossilized shells. Rufino squints his irritated eyes to gaze at the vast field of white, using his hand as a visor. The Great Saltbed stretches out before him, and he heads toward that place at the top of the mountain where the solar wind has created in the sky an aurora shaped like a floating dragon and a winged serpent that spreads its jaws wide and howls. Rufino stops and raises his pistol in the air. He has one bullet left in the barrel and fires.

One shot in the air, someone's lost.

Ancantril is startled by one shot, and then hears a second. The lieutenant draws his pistol and stands up,

"Rufino!" he exclaims.

Deus's face is swollen from sleep and he can't find his weapon.

"What's going on, Indian?" he asks.

The lieutenant picks up his saddlebag, puts the saddle on his horse, and orders, "Deus, make some more coffee for when we return. Ancatril, you better go see where those shots came from."

"It was only one shot, and it came from the north. The other was a long echo of the first shot, Lieutenant," explains Ancatril.

"I heard from a good source that they are going to shoot Rufino once we arrive at the fort," Deus remarks.

"A while back, some dogs dug up the cadaver of Soria's wife. Rufino and that woman had run off together, and it seems she had Gallic disease, but he didn't care."

"It's called syphilis," says the lieutenant.

"Anyway, Soria's not going to forgive him and will find an excuse to have him shot."

Lost in thought, the lieutenant rubs his temples with his fingers.

"I feel dizzy this morning," he says.

"Check which way Ancatril went. I have to note that in my campaign journal, but I'll do it later."

"Yes, Lieutenant."

The lieutenant mounts his horse, spurs it on, and leaves at a fast trot. The Indian rides to the north. Deus hears the sound of the horses riding away, and a melancholy feeling comes over him as he watches the flickering sunlight suddenly appear behind a hill.

The lieutenant mumbles to himself that the soldier who brought that knife showed a lot of courage searching for their campsite so he could fulfill the last wish of a dying man. He seemed to come from another time with that red armband he was wearing, or was it blue . . .

In that light, it was hard to tell what color the badge was. In spite of his shocking appearance, his gaze, steady as that of a salamander, conveyed a mysterious calm, as if he could walk through flames. The encounter left everyone confused. Perhaps he belonged to Sanabria's squadron, which had departed earlier, taking the rescued women, cattle, and confiscated belongings of the Indians.

If what the soldier said was true, then everything gained was lost in the desert, and even if he'd been a bandit, his warning should still be taken into consideration in case danger was lurking down the road.

Ancatril rides through the forest. Soon the midday sun will be high in the sky, filling the air with sizzling heat. He dismounts at the edge of the Great Saltbed and takes a few steps, crunching salt beneath his feet. His dry mouth tastes like salt as he shouts, and the wind returns his call. There's no way of knowing if anyone can hear him. Ancatril thinks that Rufino must have been crazy to have ventured into that place, and he has no intention of following him. The trail left by Rufino's boots vanishes in the salt field. A few meters away, he sees something shining against the white salt. Ancatril picks up the watch that once belonged to Ordoñez, wraps it in a handkerchief and puts it away for safekeeping. Intuition tells him someone else is out there, that they're not alone in the saltbed.

The Indian looks in all directions and doesn't see a thing, but he can't shake the feeling that someone's following them. He wonders what they want. In the desert anything's possible. In the early afternoon, the air smells like damp earth. At the border, raindrops must be falling like rocks over the sand-stone. Ancatril and his horse rush to leave the saltbed behind them.

The sky and white salt never meet on the Patagonian horizon. Shadows of the distant hills loom over the saltbed, turning the color of onyx as they wax and wane.

Rufino feels overcome by the weariness that has tempted him to escape since the first day they recruited him for the Campaign. Ever since he ran off with Soria's wife, the two of them feared that some soldier would shoot or stab them, leaving them in the desert for beasts to gnaw on their bones. God took her first, and he was left behind to bury her. Before she took her last breath, she told him not to let them kill him. Rufino turns and looks back at his footprints. He can't erase his steps or the traces they've left in the salt. Someone keeps shouting his name over and over, and he recognizes the voice of Ancatril. The Indian once told him that the ancient *Mapuches* knew the story of birds that fly without their flock because they bear a message. Rufino smiles as a flamingo glides low over the Great Saltbed, its wings spread wide. It soars above the storm, and the sound of its wings flapping can no longer be heard.

The Indian has stopped calling him. As Rufino walks further and further away from the devil's country, the salt turns pure white in the blinding light and creaks under his worn soles. He can wander around that emptiness for days without stopping, until he loses the feeling of being pursued by the law. He no longer has to serve.

Ancatril reports to the lieutenant that Rufino got lost in the saltbed and must be dead. He's about to say something else, but the lieutenant interrupts him.

"With Carranza's mysterious disappearance and now this, I don't know how I'm going to explain what happened once we get to the fort."

Disturbed, the Indian looks around and declares:

"Someone's been following us."

The lieutenant stares at him.

"Why do you say that?"

Ancatril tells him he knows the desert like the palm of his hand and can hear and see things going on there.

Deus reacts with a skeptical gesture that suggests the Indian doesn't know what he's talking about.

The lieutenant looks at both of them with disgust.

"I just want to leave this hell," he says.

"Let's get out of here."

Far from this territory eroded by salt, the air is different. The vast space of the desert spreads wide open before the weary.

Rufino walks, dragging his feet and panting. A clap of thunder rumbles. Gusts of wind let loose, and the day turns so dark that Rufino can finally gaze up at the cloudy sky. He cups his hand and sips the sweet-tasting water he captures. Raindrops make a soft sound as they hit the ground. His wet clothes weigh him down, but the rain soothes him. Rufino lies down and slowly falls asleep on the saltbed. He dreams of riding over the plain toward his destiny. He can see it on the distant horizon, but he's tired. It's not worth continuing the journey.

A subterranean river flows beneath the Great Salt Lake, and the salt absorbs the water below the surface. Rufino's uniform loses its color, leaving a dead man to rest in a pool of blue.

Lum sits on her mare a short distance from Rufino. The white ground reflects the rays of the sun. She looks at the body of the soldier lying there and feels no mercy for that dead man.

She believes justice has been served by him losing his way, pursued by his demons. Lum never touched him; she just added the *cebil* powder which opened the doors to his fears. A despicable soul sees only darkness.

The horses hesitate and plant their hooves firmly on the rocky path as they ascend single file, but the men spur them on. They've heeded the warning of the loyal soldier and changed their direction. After passing the mountain range, they'll cross the plateau. The horses dip their heads forward as they climb the slope. The mule balances the weight of its load over its nimble legs.

"That makes two deserters," Deus remarks.

"They're corpses without a coffin," replies the lieutenant.

"I bet the crows have picked what's left of them," says the photographer, staring into the distance as if he were projecting an image in his head.

"Like pieces of jerky," adds the Indian.

"We're never going to make it to the border. No one leaves this desert alive. I thought everyone knew that, Lieutenant. Rufino's lucky he's dead. It's the best thing that could've happened to him," says Deus.

"I would've like to have been there to see him face the firing squad," adds the lieutenant.

"He always had the look of a moron," Deus comments.

"I dreamed about that bloody soldier. Did you two see him?"

"He was there," replies the lieutenant. "I have the knife he gave me."

The lieutenant believes the long gaucho knife he's wearing once belonged to the Restorer of the Law.

They come across a solitary tree that was sacred to the Indians. The lieutenant wants to be photographed next to it. The ground around the enormous ancient tree has been disturbed.

"There used to be a tomb here for my people," Ancatril says.

Instead of a Christian cross, they see a pile of stones. In the staggering heat, the photographer rummages through the overturned sea of sand looking for the *Mapuche* grave. The lieutenant suggests that he bury the skulls he already has in a bag, but Deus replies it's not a question of returning them, but rather digging up others to take away and exhibit in the city.

"They've buried a chief here," says Deus.

Ancatril nods in agreement, and the helpless look on his face reveals he knows the photographer's intentions.

The *Mapuches* made special arrangements for the burial of a chief, the only one to have an individual grave with proper honors. His favorite animals would accompany him, along with some of his valuable possessions.

Deus picks up a shovel and begins to dig. After the first scoops, he discovers the bones of a horse and sets them aside. Then he finds the skeleton of a dog, pots, carved bones, corn and other grains, and finally a mummified corpse. Deus examines it, removes the silver jewelry that adorns him, and puts the treasures in his bag.

Ancatril falls to his knees when he sees the corpse, and his eyes fill with tears. He thinks he'll be plagued by a curse for having participated in the desecration of that tomb.

The lieutenant raises his hand, telling Deus to take the photograph that he requested so they can move on.

"You have to move carefully on these sand dunes," Deus points out as he rises to set up his equipment. Then he takes a portrait of the men in front of the excavated tomb. The human and animal remains and objects are the spoils of war.

It's not possible to determine the amount of time the wet plate should remain inside the dark chamber because it depends on the intensity of the light reflected on the objects being photographed at that time of day.

Lum gallops toward the slope of the mountain following the men who are about three hundred meters ahead. A toad jumps, narrowly missing the hooves of her mare, and disappears when it reaches the shadowy edge of the forest. At that moment, an old shepherd crosses in front of her with his flock of sheep, and the mare stops. Lum hadn't heard the sheep bleating or the sound of their hooves as they drew near. She's surprised to see an old *Ranquel* in the middle of the desert and asks him what he's doing there.

The old man tells her that his people live in the south and that he's come to exchange sheep for corn and wheat.

She tells him that all her people are dead, that the entire village was wiped out. The old man offers his condolences, looking down with sorrow. He tells her she can come with him and live with his tribe beyond the Colorado River, where the soldiers haven't yet invaded.

The young *machi* thanks him and says she'll go there, but she can't come with him now because she has to finish something first. The old Indian looks at her with suspicion, nods, herds his flock, and disappears.

Lum looks toward the south and then toward the west. The soldiers should have covered a lot of ground by now. She looks one way and then the other, undecided. She knows she could just cross the Colorado River instead of traveling along its shore in territory that's been appropriated. She could head for the free lands in the south but urges her mare to move on so she doesn't lose track of the men.

On nights with a full moon, the *machi* used to pick herbs near the ford of the river and taught Lum the names of the plants and how to use them. Before her mother died, Lum used to walk with her to the caves where drawings adorn the stone walls and listen to stories passed on by the elders.

There once was a time when a race of giants inhabited Patagonia. Some went off to war, and the others waited for them to return. When they realized the warriors weren't coming back, the giants cried, and that is how the chain of lagoons was formed.

Deep inside the caves there was a drawing of a woman riding after her prey with a spear in her hand.

A lump rises in Lum's throat.

Under the torrential rain and howling wind, the soaked animals descend, digging their horseshoes into the mud. The mule wobbles as it makes its way along the edge of the ledge, then slips and plunges into the void. Its heavy body and load crash about ten meters to the bottom of the cliff, and its bones snap as they break. The crate with the camera is broken to bits, the metal trays clatter, flasks of liquid gas burst and spill, and the rest of the equipment tumbles and shatters to pieces. Deus gets off his horse to peer over the cliff, sobbing as he watches his belongings disappear into the sludge. A pungent smell of ammonia rises to his nose. The contents of a flask turn to foam as it runs over salt and releases poisonous vapors that contaminate the air. Below, scattered objects sink into the mud. Coffee, flour, and rice spill out of their broken bags.

The lieutenant orders Ancatril to go down and gather the rice that spilled into the bushes. The Indian leaves Deus's side and slides down the slope. The mule stops braying when he sees him nearby. It's barely breathing, and Ancatril realizes it's in agony and can't move. It must have broken its ribs. Ancatril puts his hand on its head and speaks to him, and the wind carries words in the *Mapuche* language, *paila, paila.* The mule wags its tail slowly, and its eyes begin to close. The Indian has no doubt it's suffering, and without hesitating a moment, shoots it.

"Hurry up and gather the rice," the lieutenant shouts.

He's surrounded by hundreds of grains of rice stuck in the muddy grasses and worries about letting it all go to waste. He trudges into the mud and begins to pick up each grain, one by one, with his feet buried in the muck, but soon realizes it's a lost cause. The Indian looks up at the lieutenant hoping for new orders.

"Forget it, let's not waste any more time," he shouts down at him.

Ancatril tries to climb the slope, but can't. The mud's slippery, and the rain continues to flood the ravine, forming a stream. The water races, dragging hinges that flew off boxes, food left over from breakfast, pieces of pots and pans that smash together in a pile against a wall of mud that's collapsing.

Once again Ancatril sees the avalanche that had buried him in the bottom of the trench. He hears a roar like a wave breaking over him. His legs tremble, and suddenly everything goes dark and he can no longer see anything as he becomes wrapped in a shroud-like blanket under the cold earth.

They throw him a rope to grab and watch him from above. Ancatril's manages to tie a knot around his waist before he passes out. The lieutenant and Deus haul him up, pulling until they can lay him on the ground.

Even though her eyes can barely make out the shape of trees and objects through the downpour, Lum knows those men are out there trying to move ahead through the pass between the boulders. She sits on her mare, wrapped in a sheep's hide. Everything's enshrouded by dark clouds, illuminated only by flashes of lightning that expose the empty space where the trail seems to end in an abyss.

Beneath the shelter of an acacia tree, Lum balances nimbly on the back of her mare, then grabs the branches and climbs up the tree trunk to get a better look at what the soldiers are doing. Every move the young *machi* makes is very deliberate and barely audible in the midst of the storm.

The wind starts to blow fiercely and bears down on her, and she clings to the tree.

Not too far away, the men are struggling with the gale force wind as well. Lum keeps a close watch, waiting for them to move further ahead so she can continue pursuing them.

The landscape turns monotonous as the day lingers on. The men push forward, riding west along the Colorado River, unable to tell if it rushes toward the sea or flows upstream toward the mountains. The plain shows no sign of the passage of time, and no movement can be detected in the distance except for the flickering shadows that lengthen as the afternoon draws to an end. It seems that nothing has happened, neither a war nor a dream.

The three horsemen charge ahead, battling like arm wrestlers in an obstinate struggle to see what's stronger: the desert or their desire to reach the border. The wind observes them. They can't hear that voice calling to them:

Stay if you like, you ruminating cows, but don't chew everything in your path, and don't come here to fence in the land.

Sepúlveda

As he leaves the fort to hunt chinchillas on his day off, Sepúlveda has no way of knowing that destiny's about to deal him a bad hand.

He wears a large hat he bought at the border, a bandana tied around his neck, and a whip. His pants are secured by a leather sash, and his open shirt, with rolled-up sleeves, exposes his chest. One of his boots has a wooden heel, and he limps when he walks, dragging one leg.

He rides an Appaloosa. The chinchillas he caught are tied together and dangle in a row over the saddle.

He's ridden several leagues into the thick forest, and when he decides to return with his prey, he realizes that Indians have been following him.

He sees a lagoon a short distance away and spurs his horse on. He doesn't hesitate and plunges forward until the water reaches the horse's back, then waits there with a Remington in his hand.

About forty Indians follow their leader and appear along the ravines. They taunt him with war cries, surrounding him in relentless pursuit. They can't get close enough to spear him because Sepúlveda's aiming at them with his weapon.

The Indians are patient. They know he'll kill them instantly if they go into the water. They maintain their positions. Nothing moves at that moment, not even the wind. They wait, motionless. Sepúlveda and his horse can't hold out there for long.

Their young leader wears a silver necklace imbedded with lapis lazuli stones and carries a spear adorned with ostrich feathers where the arrowhead joins the shaft.

The soldier's horse whinnies in protest. The time has come for Sepúlveda to leave the lagoon. The leader tells him to come out, that they won't kill him, that he'll protect him.

Sepúlveda doesn't say a word.

The Indian shouts:

"You won't be the first Christian staying in my village. I have white friends, and I protect them. We raid the borders together."

Sepúlveda hesitates. He doesn't move, but his horse bucks. He's sure that Indian has cut off the heads of more men than he's offered hospitality to. He doesn't trust him, but he has no choice. If he comes out and tries to shoot them, the *Mapuches* will come at him from all sides with their horses and drive a lance right through him if he tries to escape.

When he runs out of bullets, he finally has to accept the offer. He leaves the lagoon, and the Indians surround him and waste no time leading him to the village. The band of Indians ride at a fast pace. When they hand him over, Sepúlveda doesn't resist.

Three Indians accompany him to the tent of the chief, who demands that Sepúlveda inform him of the army's maneuvers. He refuses, saying he knows nothing. The chief doesn't believe him, and the corners of his wrinkled mouth contort into a grimace. He loses his patience and gives the order to bind him and throw him into the pigsty.

Tied with barbed wire, lying in mud and filth, Sepúlveda thinks he has little time left and knows that he must invent a story that will somehow free him from the savages. He trembles in fear and feels nauseous.

He asks to speak to the chief again. When he faces him, he assures him that he'll confess everything. He tells him about the plans the army is supposedly preparing in the fort to attack the village. The chief listens to him, but tells him that he's lying and gives the order for them to spear him.

Before they kill him, as luck would have it, they send him into the forest to cut wood under the watchful eyes of a pair of Indians who bring liquor with them. After a long while, the Indians get drunk while he chops logs. When he sees them laughing uncontrollably and hears them beginning to slur their words, Sepúlveda takes advantage of the situation and pounces on them, sinking the axe into the head of one Indian and then striking a second blow to the chest of the other, leaving them lying in a pool of blood.

Sepúlveda escapes, limping because they've taken his boots. Night falls, and he tries to guide himself by the stars but gets confused by what little he knows of the sky, and in spite of all his efforts to gain his bearings, goes the wrong way. Instead of heading toward the fort, he goes in the opposite direction, walking for days, dragging his shorter leg until he gets lost on a path with no way out.

When they found him, he was nearly a corpse, his feet and arms pecked away by insects and his clothes torn to shreds by the thicket. They thought he was dead, but when they poked him with a stick, Sepúlveda let out a groan and opened his eyes.

Deus

The horses gallop against the wind on that desolate path full of rubble and holes. The men ride in silence as they approach the fort, no more than ten leagues away. Even so, it seems as if they're stuck in the same point, frozen in the middle of the desert. Deus speaks, even though the lieutenant may not be listening to him:

"You know, Lieutenant, I wanted to return to Buenos Aires so much, but now I'm reluctant to finish that journey. I've come to feel farther from home here than when I was in Paris. We're a little more savage now than before, don't you think? The thought of leaving this place wears me out because when I get to the city, I'll have to mount a farce that will please my parents and convince them they should pay for another ticket to send me back to Marseille. My poor mother. I'm all she has. She'd love to see me married, but I never imagined that life for myself. I don't have friends anymore in Buenos Aires. Many are married with children and live off their family name. I've nothing in common with them. You must have realized, Lieutenant, that I want something else for myself. I don't want to go on pretending."

Deus pauses for a second before continuing.

"And my father, wrapped in his cashmere throw, with his kidskin gloves and aristocratic prejudices, is so aloof. For him, reflection is a waste of time. They serve him tea on the terrace at five o'clock in the afternoon, no matter what's happening, and he still thinks I was in Paris studying law.

I'll have to pretend some more, sit across from my father and smoke my pipe, ask the servants to bring me a drink, and tell him about our victory and the mysteries of Patagonia.

"The war hasn't changed me. It's the desert that's changed me, the desert that's driven us crazy and made us lose our sense of time and distance. It devours our equipment and the little bit of civilization in us. Civilization isn't possible here. You have to keep moving to find a way out and stay alert so they don't find you later with empty eye sockets.

"I'm not going to fritter away my life anymore measuring patches of land and writing documents for the homeland. I'm going to go back to France and live the way I want to live. and I'll buy an astrometer and gaze at the sky. Last night I dreamed about an open door."

May 26, 1879

Mon cher journal,

Yesterday I had a dream in the early hours of dawn, but I better not share with the others what I saw. I was in a basement and had a key in my hand. In front of me was a door, and when I went to put the key in the lock, the door opened on its own. Inside were bodies of headless women dangling from hooks. I slammed the door shut, and the word "oppression" suddenly appeared before me.

When the war ends, not even we victors will have triumphed over those unnameable forces of creation and destruction. War ignites the fire and devours the dead, but something even more sinister burns in the underworld. Oppression is the word, and that is war. We'll never conquer the devil's country, not with miles of barbed wire or force. Buenos Aires, now that dawn's about to break and the opaline mist rises over the river, I think that when I return to your shore, perhaps I won't be the same anymore. Perhaps the ravages of time make us grow until we become men. I'm going to miss the stars that flow into this heavenly vault, over the vast expanse of savage silence. But war has stirred the melancholy of a foreigner in me, and autumn makes me feel old. Solitude is now my home.

S. Deus

Lum rides until she comes to a stream. Exhausted, starving, and aching all over, she gets off her mare. Fatigue and little sleep have left dark circles under her eyes. While the mare drinks, she bathes herself, relishing the touch of the flowing water.

A few meters from the shore, she sees a crow fighting with a crossed pit viper. The bird flaps its wings and pecks at its prey as the viper straightens half its body, ready to attack. The crow is faster, and before the serpent can strike, grabs it with its beak behind the venomous head. The crow takes flight and releases it, and the snake falls, spinning in the air until it crashes against the ground. The bird swoops down and devours it.

The young *machi* also needs to hunt something to eat. Her provisions have run out and she hasn't found wild fruit anywhere. Lum kneels down at an angle between two large rocks where the current is deepest. She stays still and alert. Suddenly she makes a quick movement with her arms and grabs a silvery fish out of the water. It tries to slip away, but she holds it firmly, taking long strides to get out of the stream. She throws the fish onto the shore and watches as it flops around until its gills close. Lum cuts off its head with her knife, scrapes the scales, deftly removes the guts, and then eats it raw.

Lying on the shore, she falls into a deep slumber, while the crow scavenges in the sand for the last remains of the snake.

In Lum's dream, leaves quiver and trees rise tall and sway. The wind with its powerful force strikes the branches, and its precise blows threaten to uproot one of the most ancient calden trees. Lum's afraid to hear the sacred tree creak and crash if it falls. Nothing seems to divert her attention from that giant. She tries to shake off the dream and escape the nightmare that disturbs her. She speaks to the tree for a long while, imploring it to stand tall:

Foike, don't fall now, I need to drink your sap. You're the reason for my journey, my guardian spirit. Without your protection, I don't know what I'll do. Foike, don't fall, don't.

Lum awakens in a daze, her ears still ringing.

That night it was Deus's turn to stand guard.

He writes in his diary:

In the end that mule was so loaded down it couldn't handle the weight, and that's why I lost everything.

We were attacked by a pack of hungry dogs that barked at us, frothing at the mouth with their tongues hanging out. We shot at them and they scattered, howling in fear. They caused us great harm running off with the salted and cured meat that would have fed us for three days. The Indians eat their own dogs in dire times.

Deus flinches when he sees what appears to be a silhouette on the other side of the campfire. He gets up and walks through the bushes with his gun cocked. He hears footsteps and stops to look around, ready to shoot.

He thinks he sees a woman watching him. Deus feels uneasy, but before he can react, a mare crosses in front of the figure and gallops off, vanishing into the trees. He stares in that same direction, beyond which lies only the desert. Nervous, he ventures into the brush as if drawn by a magnet.

In the midst of an eerie light, he sees a girl of medium height standing with her feet covered by the mist hovering over the grassland. Her threadbare wool tunic is barely visible through the wild grasses that rise nearly two meters tall.

Deus makes a gesture, and is about to say something, but Lum signals him to be quiet, as if confiding in him. He follows her and doesn't take his eyes off the girl as she approaches and then stops.

"Who are you? Where do you come from?"

She doesn't respond.

"Are you lost?"

Lum remains silent.

Deus takes a step forward and sees her light-colored eyes.

"You're not a full-bred Indian."

He takes another long step and stands before her. He puts his fingers under Lum's chin and lifts it a bit to get a better look at her.

The young *machi* stares at him.

"Your face is fascinating, a blend . . ."

Lum is faster than his words, and before Deus can get over his admiration, she removes the knife from her sash and grasping it sideways with a firm hand, slashes his throat. Lum's vision becomes cloudy, and in the red deluge that washes over her, she sees her father wielding his saber, drawing a sweeping semi-circle in the air that ends at the point where her mother's head is severed from her body, the very point from which Deus's blood springs forth.

Hold onto the head so it doesn't roll.

Deus tries to cover the gash on his neck with his hands.

Lum stands there as if seeing it all for the first time, and in that confusion of images, she suddenly drops the knife and runs away.

Deus attempts to drag himself to the campsite. Death allows him to reach the spot where the lieutenant is sleeping. He calls out to him with what's left of his voice. The lieutenant awakens to the sight of Deus's face with its now vacant eyes.

February 19, 1879

Mon cher journal,

I have to admit this savage desert possesses a voluptuous beauty.

I don't believe I've ever smelled the aroma of flowers so intensely and in such an intimate way as I have in these days. The withered flowers are carried by the wind and make me sneeze by the campfire. I'd never allow anyone to read this diary because I'm not a writer. During these last days, I've renounced my duties as a surveyor as well. I'm just a humble photographer, and after revealing what I can about these lands, I don't wish to return.

S. Deus

Another Life

Lum runs until she falls, exhausted, heaving and vomiting, even though she has little in her stomach. Then she rolls onto her back and cries.

Five years ago she was on the riverbank covered in blood and shaking, when the shadow of an old woman fell upon her. It was the *machi* who had come to look for medicinal herbs and came across the scene of destruction. The old *machi* wrapped Lum in her poncho, and the warm embrace helped calm her down until she fell asleep.

The *machi* whispered a sacred chant in her ear. Lum opened her eyes and said:

I'll be a machi *and will heal the sick. You came to give me a new life.*

When a young girl is chosen by the great celestial spirit to be a *machi*, a celebration takes place, and everyone dances and bestows their blessings. They pray to Ngenechen to offer her animals and a strong soul, a knife and bamboo spear to ward off the harmful spirits.

Even though the *machi* knew that many would not accept Lum's initiation, the chief appreciated that mysterious light the young girl harbored, a light that belongs only to the shamans.

She was always different, not just because of the white blood coursing through her veins. The people of the village used to say she was cursed because of the way her father had killed her mother and that deception lurked behind her gaze.

The majority rejected her, and yet the *machi* told them she was certain Lum could pass the great trial.

A *machi* can see herself as a skeleton. She can come back to life and be born again in a mystical way.

Lum felt her mother inside her from the moment she embraced her dead body on the shore of the river. But now it was time to let her go so that her own skeleton could survive alone. The spirit of her mother needed to return to its origins, find its resting place, and from that moment on, begin its journey.

The sky is cloudy and dawn has yet to break. Off in the distance, Lum can see a thick gray cloud moving and imagines that the mountains are coming to meet her.

It will take another week for the wounds on her arms and legs to heal. To forget the pain, she focuses her attention on the spirits that remained wandering after the fire. She knows that only she can help them and that without the *cultrún*, she will have to double her efforts so that they may rest in peace.

Lum crawls into the brush to hide. The grasses are yellow. She remembers that the *machi* used to say to her:

Look Lum how the light of the sun changes. Let its radiance shine in you.

At that moment, an invisible hand from above gently lifts her beyond the clouds, and she becomes light as a feather. Energy enters her body in a constant stream, and she senses that she's part of something immense and alive.

She'd like to stay there floating forever, but the hand grasps her again and leads her back to the ground, where she lands softly among the bushes.

Lum smiles knowing that Ngenechen has been her guide and that she is now a powerful *machi*.

1864

The white man stood there fascinated as he watched her kneading clay and decided to make a trade. She was twelve years old and he was thirty-six.

The man went to her father's house and told him that he wanted to trade a ten-kilo bag of flour for his daughter. At first the father refused, but after the other insisted, he told him he'd have to think about it because what he offered was very little. He should give him at least three bags. The white man laughed and let him know he had no other option than to accept. The Indian spoke a few sentences in *Mapuche,* raising his voice, and left his house, returning a few minutes later with Fén.

The man smiled when he saw her and handed over the bag. The deal was sealed with a handshake, and he took her away.

Fén spent all her time tending to the white man. She sheared the sheep and molded the clay. He'd bought her as if she were an object, and like pouring salt on a wound, he'd shout at her over and over that she wasn't worth more than a bag of flour, even to her father. The Indian would remain silent. One glare from that *huinco* was enough to devastate her.

They lived like that for a while, him abusive and Fén impervious to that monstrous shadow that swept over her, trying to humiliate her. He missed the comforts of the city, which made him even more irritable and intolerant toward the customs of the Indians, and he'd unload his hatred on Fén, insulting her.

One night the white man entered the hut, and when he saw her wrapped in her shawl, blinded by fury, he beat her until she lost consciousness.

Boredom drove him to leave suddenly, abandoning her with a two-and -a-half-year-old daughter whom he barely distinguished from the rest of the girls in the tribe.

The white man rode off without stopping, leaving the desert behind. He wanted to go back to his world and see if he could recover the life he'd led before coming to the village.

In Buenos Aires, some of his relatives gave him a cold reception. No one was pleased with his presence, and although the authorities were no longer after him, his reputation preceded him. Rumors spread that he'd acquired the ways of the savages.

He began to get together with old friends and spend money in bars and brothels, but that distraction didn't last long. The man who'd pressed charges for swindling him crossed his path one night when he was returning home and took justice into his own hands, stabbing him and leaving him lying on the street.

The white man survived and eventually his wounds healed, but he was alone and missed the attention the Indian girl had given him.

Six years passed before the white man returned to the village to lay claim to the Indian.

 During those years, Fén had made a living from her work, managing on her own with strength and tenacity. Her daughter was nearly nine years old and helped her mother with all the chores.

The white man arrived unexpectedly one afternoon when Fén and her little girl were weaving on the loom. He told the woman she belonged to him and that she should go with him and leave her daughter in the village.

Upon hearing those words, the girl started to cry. The white man tried to shut her up, turning toward her and raising his hand, but in that moment, Fen intervened so that he wouldn't touch her.

She told her daughter everything would be fine, then looked at the white man and consented with a nod of her head.

That night while the *huinca* was sleeping, Fén woke the girl up and signaled for her to be quiet. She grabbed a satchel that held some provisions, and they fled.

They couldn't travel fast by foot, and Fén prayed that destiny would be on their side. They'd walked a couple kilometers when she heard the galloping of a horse coming towards them. She told her daughter to run, and tripping over rocks, they searched for a place to hide. There was nothing in the desert, no place to disappear.

With each second she heard the pounding hooves getting closer, and she felt trapped. The air whipped her face. She hadn't noticed how strong the wind was until it abruptly stopped, thirty seconds of total stillness in which the world seemed to come to a halt. Fén knew it was a bad sign when the wind suddenly stopped. She saw a *canelo* tree ahead of them and tried to hide behind it, but the trunk barely concealed them.

The sound of hooves was closing in on them, and Fén mustered up courage and ran again, holding the girl by the hand, but the white man caught up with them.

He reined his horse to a stop right in front of them, dismounted, and without saying a word, grabbed her by the arm. The Indian knew she couldn't fight that man. She mounted the horse, holding on tight to her daughter who clung to her. He climbed on behind them and took hold of the reins. Fén could feel his tense body against her, and he didn't need to say a word for her to know he was furious.

When they got to the hut, the man shoved them inside and forced them to lie down.

The next morning Fén didn't see him or his belongings anywhere. She thought that he'd left or was sorry he'd come back for her, and a sense of relief made her body relax. She prepared something to eat and then took her daughter to the river to bathe.

The little girl dunked her head under the water and opened her eyes to look at the fish, while her mother watched her. She raised her head and spit out a little fish she'd caught in her mouth, making her mother laugh and think that all that had happened the day before had been a bad dream.

It was at that moment that Fén heard the neighing of a horse and turned around. The expression on her face changed when she saw the silhouette of the white man against the bright sunlight. He'd halted his horse and was sitting in the saddle watching them from the hilltop.

Sauce Chico River, 1852

The road borders the river. One of its streams makes a turn and moves slowly like a blue vein. The lieutenant hears the sound of a cart approaching and his father's voice, but it's his own voice coming from far away that asks, "Father, do you believe in life after this one?"

"Hard to know if that exists, son."

It's the last day of his visit to Bahía Blanca, to the same humble house by the dock.

"What are you looking at?"

"I'm looking out the window and see a ship docked at the port, Father, but no one's on deck."

The hooves of the horses pulling the cart resound.

"Did you ever see that Indian girl again, Father?" the lieutenant asked.

"That's another story," he answered. "You weren't even one year old when you fell from that cart."

And he told him again about that frantic race to find him. It was nearly dark, and the girl was waiting by the bridge of the Sauce Chico River, certain that someone would come for him. She was holding him in her arms and had let him suck her nipple so he wouldn't cry. The Indian girl returned the boy to his father, who simply thanked her.

The lieutenant puts his finger in his mouth and conjures the taste of seawater before turning once again to gaze at the fine dust hovering over the river.

Resurrection

Ghosts

A man approaches on horseback in the midst of a cloud of dust. It's the lieutenant. The die has been cast, and Lum doesn't try to escape. The lieutenant goes over to her and sees that her wool tunic is as bloody as a butcher's.

"Where did you come from, Indian?"

He dismounts and approaches her with caution, and after seeing that she doesn't resist, he ties her wrists with straps. Then he lifts the girl over the rump of the animal, mounts behind her, and urges his horse on. He rides seated near its hindquarters, his chest forward, his arms tense, and the reins loose. When he digs his spurs into the horse's flesh, it neighs and takes longer strides, as blood trickles down its sides. The sunlight fades in and out over the plain.

The lieutenant thinks he sees the outline of a ship made of spiderwebs and bones gliding through the sand dunes in search of a place to dock. The ship has no crew and no one is on deck. Adrift, its sails billow as it glides off into a dazzling light that quickly grows dim.

"I'm going crazy," the lieutenant thinks to himself.

Lum clings to the horse's mane.

Fear rules over death, no more savage screams, no more battles. Hardly any Indians remain in the desert.

"Fence in with barbed wire? What for? Conquer? What for?" murmurs the lieutenant.

Lum, the lieutenant, and Ancatril continue the journey along the detour they took a few kilometers back when the bloody horseman warned them of danger. They enter into a strange territory where neither Indians nor soldiers normally venture, a trail that leads nowhere, making it difficult to reach the fort.

On one side, between two rows of locust trees, they see a path leading to an iron gate that protects an old estate.

The lieutenant has Lum on his mare and stops when he catches a glimpse of the house standing about one hundred fifty meters to the right of them.

They're not that far from the fort, but as if he wishes to delay their arrival, the lieutenant tells Ancatril that they're going to see if someone's there, and perhaps they'll allow them to wash up.

They go down the path and arrive at the padlocked gate. The lieutenant claps his hands and shouts.

"Is anyone here?"

After a few minutes, a man about sixty years old and armed with a rifle peers out and asks what they want.

The lieutenant introduces himself, tells him that he's in the army, that they're headed for the fort, and hoped to find some hospitality in that house.

The man stares at the medals hanging from the lieutenant's jacket and immediately asks why he's bringing those Indians with him.

"One's my soldier and the other's a hostage," he says.

The old man lowers his firearm, opens the lock, and lets them in.

They enter the large house, which has long hallways and thick walls. The expensive furniture, the marble staircase, and the moth-eaten velvet drapes tell a story of past splendor. Intrigued, the lieutenant asks if the owners had been frightened off by a band of Indians.

The old man shakes his head no.

"They were bandits, political enemies of the master. They came one night fifty years ago, murdered everyone, and ran off with the cattle."

They go down a hallway that leads to an inner courtyard with a well. The lieutenant asks if he can bathe himself with clean water from the cistern. The old man agrees and lowers the wooden bucket to fill it with water. Enthused by the prospect of speaking with someone, he continues.

"Relatives of the deceased owner lived here for a while, but they left in a rush because they said the place was haunted. Later, the heirs of the family contracted me to take care of the place. I'm the second caretaker. The first one died of a heart attack one stormy night."

The old man observes the three visitors. None of them seem alarmed. Disappointed by the impact of his words, he raises the bucketful of water and proceeds.

"It's just the wind that batters the doors and slips through the cracks around the windows, but those people believed they were hearing voices of the dead."

The man pauses and says that his ranch is behind the main house, next to the cemetery where the remains of the murdered family rest.

He lifts the bucket from the well's hook and walks toward an open door at the other side of the courtyard.

"Follow me."

The lieutenant accompanies Lum, whose hands are tied, and Ancatril walks behind, carrying a rifle.

The caretaker leads them up some steps, and once they're upstairs, they walk across a veranda with archways. The colonnade leads to a room with a bathtub into which the old man empties the water.

"I can offer you bread and wine, Lieutenant," he says and leaves the room to fill the bucket again.

The lieutenant gives the order to Ancatril to take Lum to the courtyard and guard her while he bathes.

The Indian obeys and shoves the young *machi*. They cross the veranda and go down the stairs. They've taken a wrong turn and can't find the place from which they came. Ancatril looks around, confused.

"It should be through here," he says in his native tongue, as they go down a hallway where several family portraits hang.

Lum can't resist staring at the paintings of those white people. They seem to return her gaze, as if they wished to tell her something. She stops to look at a little girl who extends a hand to her in a gesture of terror, as if trying to escape the golden frame. Ancatril can't see what the *machi* sees and grabs her by the arm to keep moving.

They go out to a patio behind the house. The grass is tall and neglected, and in front of it there's a chicken coop and what was once a stable.

Lum sees the girl from the painting standing in front of them, wearing a pink dress with three tiers of ruffles, white socks trimmed in lace, and her hair tied with a silk ribbon. She's pointing with her index finger at the chicken coop. Lum shoves Ancatril, catching him off guard, and runs to where the girl is pointing. Ancatril follows and grabs her by the arm again.

She sees a small, worn-out shoe in the dust behind the chicken wire where the hens are kept. She opens the gate and picks up the shoe, and the scene unfolds before her. There are four children hiding in the chicken coop, among them the little girl who called out to her from the painting. She sees them terrified, huddled close together. Suddenly a man comes in, the children scream, and everything turns black.

Ancantril speaks to her in the *Mapuche* language, warning her not to try to escape. Lum turns around, looks at him sternly and the Indian doesn't say another word.

"They killed innocent children here," she declares. "This time it was the whites against whites."

Lum demands that Ancatril return the *cultrún* to her that the lieutenant took away. She tells him that not long ago she was initiated as a *machi* and that the drum the lieutenant stole is her only inheritance.

"There are spirits here that need to depart, Ancatril."

The Indian looks at her, and hesitates.

"I'm not going to do you any harm," Lum assures him.

Ancatril is persuaded and agrees but takes precautions before leaving and ties her to the barbed-wire fence with rope.

He returns with the *cultrún*, unties her, but doesn't put down his rifle for even a moment.

Lum beats the drum, calling out to those children, stirring feelings in Ancatril as he listens. The young *machi* performs a ceremony to guide the spirits who have stayed behind, lost in that forsaken place. As a *machi*, she is the only one who can do this. For a few minutes she concentrates on the rhythm of the drum, and her eyes turn blank as she enters a trance.

The spirit of the *machi* must depart the body during its astral trip, penetrate a virgin jungle, climb a mountain, cross seas, rivers, and swamps, until it comes in contact with the gods. All this transpires in a matter of minutes.

Vibrations resound inside the chicken coop. Ancatril and Lum are caught up in the mystery of the ritual. When she beats the drum for the last time, she pauses and opens her eyes.

Ancatril goes over to her and asks her to put her hands behind her, and he ties them again. He's hung the *cultrún* over her back.

This time they have no trouble finding the courtyard, and they sit on the ground to wait for the lieutenant to come down.

A deep calm envelops the estate.

Arrival at the Fort

Tallow candles burn in the lanterns, illuminating the frontier post. It's a puzzling construction made of adobe bricks, with no windows, not even a skylight to look out, only an opening way up high and a ladder screwed to the floor. A soldier stands in front of the door chewing tobacco, his feet firmly planted on the ground and his rifle slung over his shoulder. Sparks fly from the torches, and wisps of smoke fill the air with a musty smell. Surrounded by a ditch, the fort is a stark structure that rises from the prairie and languors in obscure idleness.

Inside the notes of an accordion can be heard.

Horses draw near at full gallop, pounding the plain. Someone's coming.

The guard leans against the door protecting the threshold. A shaft of light appears before him when he ignites the wick of a lamp. When he turns, one side of his face is illuminated.

The riders stop and get off their horses, tying them to the rings mounted on the façade. The dogs sniff at the horses' legs.

"Calm down, they're not Indians. Tiger come here," says the guard to a big brown dog who comes over wagging his tail. He lowers his ears and blinks, and sits at the guard's side. The pack disperses.

The guard clicks his heels and salutes.

The lieutenant says, "Evening, soldier, we're from the Sanabria brigade. Allow us to enter."

"I have orders not to let anyone pass."

"We're the rearguard of the division coming from the attack on the village, and we're tired. Let us in."

The soldier gives it some thought.

"Are you looking for Colonel Soria?"

"No. I have something to turn over to the general."

The guard opens the door as quickly as he closes it. He climbs the ladder and can be seen in the guard tower. A few minutes later he comes down the ladder and returns with some papers in his hand.

"What is your name?"

"Lieutenant Marcial Obligado, third regiment of the calvary."

The guard searches for the name on the first sheet.

"It's not here."

"There must be a mistake," says the lieutenant.

The soldier eyes Lum from head to toe.

"And that *china*? Soria will take a liking to that Indian girl."

No one says anything.

"Oh, look, here it is, Obligado. You're on the list of the deceased."

"Can it be that all of you are good for nothing?" says the lieutenant.

"I can't let you in," insists the guard.

"I don't know if you're trying to be some kind of joker or if you're just a fool, but this is no way to treat an officer who's traveled a long way across the desert. I've lost my entire squadron, everyone except for this Indian you see here. I'm bringing this *mestiza* as my prisoner. We're going to execute her for killing one of my men."

The lieutenant looks at the Indian girl,

"And perhaps she had something to do with the death of the other men."

"Are you telling me this half-breed finished off your men? What kind of squadron were you commanding, Lieutenant?"

The soldier goes over to Lum, whose hands are tied, and runs a hand over her face. The young *machi* lowers her head quickly and bites two fingers.

The guard screams and tries to get loose, but she doesn't release the prey from her jaws.

The lieutenant approaches Lum from behind, removes the knife from his waist, the one engraved with the initials J.M.R., and grabs her with his left hand. She opens her eyes wide and lets go of the guard, who's crouching now and howling in pain because one of his fingers is broken.

The lieutenant raises the knife in the air, but when he moves to stab her in the neck, he hesitates and freezes. Ancatril steps forward and, for the first time, brings himself to take action, rushing at the lieutenant and grabbing him by the wrists, making him drop the knife. Lum takes off running. The lieutenant shoves Ancatril, raises his Remington, and aims at the young *machi*.

Lum runs as fast as she can and sees something moving on the horizon. It's her mare galloping toward her.

The lieutenant fires. A tremor runs through Lum's body all the way to her head. A bullet has struck her ear, shearing it off.

She doesn't stop. She presses forward tenaciously, encouraged by the shouts of a powerful voice reverberating in her skull. Some drops of blood run down her neck, speckling the desert with flecks of red.

She hears the old *machi* singing in her ear:

Flesh rots over time, but not the voice.

Lum mounts her mare, and her silhouette recedes into the cold mist.

The lieutenant screams at Ancatril,

"Why did you interfere?"

"Kill me if you want," he responds.

"This Indian's a traitor! Take him to Colonel Soria," demands the soldier guarding the door.

The lieutenant doesn't respond as he gazes into the void.

"Do you hear me?" asks the soldier who's seated, cradling his wounded hand.

The lieutenant thinks that so much blood has been shed to transform the desert into what? He stands there looking at the fort, takes a deep breath as if he needs one before he can proceed. A strange chill runs through his body. He has a glazed look in his eyes. He quickly draws his pistol and fires a shot that leaves a perfect hole in the middle of the guard's forehead.

"They're going to shoot you, Lieutenant," Ancatril remarks.

The lieutenant's mouth grimaces slightly as he drops his weapon.

The desert falls silent.

Epuyén, Patagonia, 1895

I know I was born in the autumn of 1865. My mother told me that the machi washed me
with rain water on that day. My father had come from the Capital and lived among the Indians
for a while. He'd run away from his people for some reason. Perhaps he'd killed a man or was
a deserter, I don't know.

Back then the Indians of our villages prepared themselves for war and protected the low-
lands. Once a day they met to plan their moves, displaying their spears, knives, bolas, and stolen
swords and pistols. Resolute, the men patted the rumps of their mares, then stood still in silence.
Every afternoon I'd see the Indians get ready for battle at the edge of the forest. I barely remember
my father's face. One time he lifted me up to his face by my waist and looked at me like I was
a sick hen.

My mother looked like a woman of clay. She wore a copper necklace with feathers, and
her hands were always covered in mud. Every four moons, the potters of the village would go to
where the rivers join together, and they'd take me with them. We'd return with the mules laden
with stones for our work.

All that's left of the village where our huts once stood are three ancient calden trees. They
were messengers of the rain, and we had to sing to them to make the corn blossom. As long as
we sang, the ears of corn always grew strong, but now all that is lost in the desert.

Epuyén, Patagonia, 1932

My mother was called Lum Hué, and she was a machi. *She was an adult when she came to this community alone from the north. She came to heal the sick, and when she performed rituals, her words would rise amidst spirals of smoke, soaring above the highlands. I'd play, splashing in the mud or chasing goats through the thicket.*

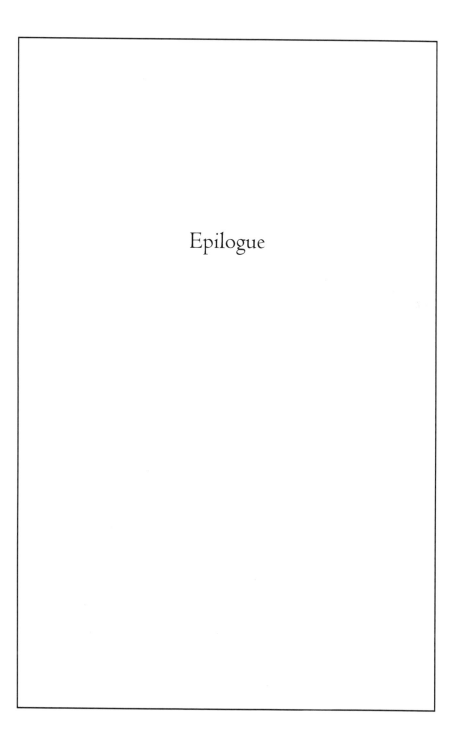

Epilogue

The Border

The desert extends its transparent nets, and dew condenses on them and spies on the living with its infinite eyes.

There's a lunar eclipse, and the sky disappears under low clouds where it meets the earth. It seems as if dawn will break at any moment, but night is falling quickly, as if the shutter of Solomon Deus's photographic machine had captured the space and time of that inconsequential scene.

Three tiny silhouettes walk slowly across the *pampa*, and though it seems that they make no progress, eventually they arrive at a small fort.

A fist bangs on the door with three resounding knocks, disturbing the stillness of the night. In the torchlight, Lum's face seems even smaller. Ancatril stands close to her and the lieutenant, as if there were no other destiny than that one, waiting for someone to open the door to them.

The door of the fort opens, and a tall man with copper-colored skin weathered by the sun crosses the threshold. He's wearing a poncho and an open shirt and holds a bottle of anise in his hand. He greets them and takes a swig.

The hinges creak when the door closes behind him.

The lieutenant points his Remington at the man.

"Take it easy, don't shoot," says the stranger, adding, "I have a Remington too, but I'm not taking aim."

"I thought you weren't a soldier," the lieutenant says.

"Yes, I am."

The man puts the bottle on the floor and keeps speaking.

"You left here a long time ago, Lieutenant. Just remember, years have gone by, and no one remembers you in this place. Leave while there's still time."

"Who are you?" the lieutenant asks.

"I'm Corporal Francisco Sepúlveda. Haven't you heard them speak of me?"

The lieutenant glances at him out of the corner of his eye, studying him.

"How strange," remarks Sepúlveda without hiding his indignation.

"Around these parts, I'm a hero, but no one cares. I've been forgotten. Some say that I lie, but the truth is I'm a survivor. Sometimes I leave the fort, walking hundreds of leagues with my bad leg, and a few days later I make it back to my point of departure. You know, in Patagonia there are places where you can barely survive for a minute. It's not wise for anyone to stay there alone, isn't that right, *china*?"

Lum doesn't seem to notice his presence.

Sepúlveda turns to the lieutenant again.

"You drink anise?"

The lieutenant wants a drink, puts away his weapon, and takes the Indian's flask as it's handed to him. The flask is empty but still smells like rum.

"*Caña* from Puán," says the corporal when he takes out the cork.

A crow hovers over their heads, unnerving them.

The black bird rests on Lum's shoulder and cackles. She smiles.

The lieutenant takes a swallow. The man continues.

"Be wary of crows. At the river crossing, there's one that always visits a sleeping cow, resting on its back and pecking at its head. It picks off the ticks, but the cow awakens with the sockets of its eyes empty."

"We know about that," says the lieutenant as he adjusts his pants.

Sepúlveda thinks he recognizes something on the lieutenant's belt and brings a torch over to get a closer look.

"What are you looking at?" reacts the lieutenant.

Sepúlveda reads out loud the letters J. M. R. engraved on the knife the lieutenant carries at his waist.

"Something very valuable. It once belonged to the Restorer of the Laws. That's not just any knife you have there," he tells him.

The lieutenant is startled by the sound of galloping horses approaching, getting louder. Men on horseback loom before them, wearing red scarves around their necks, and singing:

"*. . . He who with savages has relations, the club and a slit throat for such sedition. May the necks of savages be played like violins by the Holy Office of the Federation.*"

"Don't worry so much about them, Lieutenant. Remember that God pursues his enemies until he's through with them, and here we've all been handed over. There are no reds or blues, no skin is dark or white. We don't consider ourselves savages or civilized, because when all is said and done, what are we?"

"Are we dead?" Ancatril asks.

"It's cold. Let's not waste any more time outside here. You're tired. Come in. I'm going to tell you a story," says the corporal as he opens the door for them.

A few luminous points flicker in the distance like fireflies. They are the eyes of the watchful desert, and for those who gaze upon it, everything is obscure.

The Author

Perla Suez was born in Córdoba, Argentina, but lived the first fifteen years of her life in Basavilbaso in the province of Entre Ríos, a crucial period that informs her narrative fiction. She received a university degree in literature from the Universidad Nacional de Córdoba, Argentina, and was awarded fellowships from the French government, which enabled her to work and study from 1976-1978 at the Centro Internacional de Estudios Pedagógicos de Sèvres, during the first years of the dictatorship (1976-1983). She began her literary career publishing novels and short stories for children and was the founding director of CEDILIJ (Centro de Difusión e Investigación de Literatura Infantil y Juvenil), a center for children's literature in Córdoba. Her novel *Memorias de Vladimir* (Alfaguara, 1992) was awarded the White Ravens Prize, and has been published in several subsequent editions, most recently in 2019 by the Editorial Comunicarte. In 2000, she made her debut in the realm of adult fiction with the publication of *Letargo*, which was a finalist for the prestigious Rómulo Gallegos Prize. Since then, her popular award-winning children's novels and books have appeared in new editions and her novels for adults have been published in translations and new editions. Her first three novels written for adults (*Letargo*, *El arresto*, and *Complot*) were published individually, and in 2006, combined into one volume entitled *Trilogía de Entre Ríos* (Editorial Norma), to coincide with the publication of the English translation, *The Entre Ríos Trilogy: Three Novels.* In 2008, *Trilogía de Entre Ríos* was awarded the Primer Premio Internacional Grinzane Covour. In 2007, she won a Guggenheim Fellowship for her novel *La pasajera* (Editorial Norma, 2008), which was translated to English as *Dreaming of the Delta.* In 2013, she received the Argentine National Novel Prize for *Humo rojo* (Editorial Edhasa, 2012). In 2015, her novel *El país del diablo* received the Sor Juana Inés de la Cruz Literature Prize. In 2019, she published the novel *Furia del invierno* (Editorial Edhasa) to much critical acclaim, and also *Aconcagua* (Editorial Ojoreja), a book of short stories that won the 2018 Concurso de Proyectos Editoriales del Fondo de las Artes. Her works have been translated to English, French, Greek, Italian, Macedonian, and Serbian.

The Translator

Rhonda Dahl Buchanan is a Distinguished Teaching Professor of Spanish and Director of Latin American and Latino Studies at the University of Louisville. She is the author of numerous articles on contemporary Latin American writers and the editor of a book of critical essays, *El río de los sueños: Aproximaciones críticas a la obra de Ana María Shua* (2001). Her many translations include: *The Entre Ríos Trilogy* (University of New Mexico Press, 2006) and *Dreaming of the Delta* (Texas Tech University Press, 2014), four novels by Perla Suez. Her translation *Quick Fix: Sudden Fiction by Ana María Shua* (White Pine Press, 2008) is a bilingual illustrated anthology of microfictions. She is the recipient of a 2006 NEA Literature Fellowship for the translation of Alberto Ruy-Sánchez's novel *The Secret Gardens of Mogador: Voices of the Earth* (White Pine Press, 2009). In 2014, White Pine Press published her translation *Poetics of Wonder: Passage to Mogador* by Alberto Ruy-Sánchez, with support from Mexico's PROTRAD translation program.